# Martin Birck's Youth

# Martin Birck's Youth

Hjalmar Söderberg

*Translated by David Barrett*

Translated from the Swedish *Martin Bircks ungdom*

Published by David Barrett
*contact via www.onlineclarity.co.uk*

Paperback ISBN 978-1-5168-1511-1

Also available as a Kindle ebook, ASIN B00QZGRGDW

The front cover shows *Artillerigatan i vinterskrud* (Artillery Street in Winter Garb), 1892, by Alf Wallander (1862–1914).

# I

# The Old Street

Martin Birck was a little child who lay dreaming in his bed.

It was twilight on a summer evening, a quiet green twilight, and Martin was walking holding his mother's hand in a large, strange garden, where the shadows lay dark in the depths of the avenues. On both sides of the way grew peculiar blue and red flowers; they swayed back and forth in the wind on slender stalks. He walked and held his mother's hand and looked with surprise at the flowers and thought about nothing. "You must only pick the blue flowers, the red ones are poisonous," said his mother. Then he let go of her hand and stopped to pick a flower for her: a big blue flower it was he wanted to pick, standing nodding heavily on its stalk. What a strange flower! He looked at it and smelled it. And he looked at it once more with big, surprised eyes: of course it wasn't blue at all, it was red. It was completely red! And such a disgusting, poisonous red! He threw the vile flower on the ground and stamped on it as if on a dangerous animal. But when he turned around his mother was gone. "Mummy," he cried, "where are you? Where are you? Why are you hiding from me?" Martin ran on a little down the path but he saw no one, and he was close to tears. The avenue was quiet and empty, and it was getting darker and darker. Finally he heard a voice very near by: "Here I am, Martin, can't you see me?" But Martin saw nothing. "But here I am, just here, why don't you come over here?" Now Martin understood: just behind the elder bush — that was where the voice was coming from, he hadn't grasped that at first . . . And he ran there and looked; he was sure his mother had hidden herself there. But behind the elder bush stood Franz from the Long Terrace, grinning hideously with his fat, cracked lips and sticking out his tongue as far as he could! And such a tongue he had: it grew longer and longer, indeed, there was no end to it, and it was covered in little yellow-green blisters.

Franz was a little ruffian who lived on the Long Terrace, just across the street from Martin. Last Sunday he'd spat on Martin's new brown jacket and called him a snob.

Martin wanted to run away, but stood as if nailed to the spot. He felt his legs going numb beneath him. And the garden and the flowers and the trees were gone, and he was standing alone with Franz in a dark corner of the yard at home, by the dustbin, and he tried to scream, but he felt as if his throat were laced up tight . . .

2

But when he woke up his mother was standing next to the bed with a clean white shirt in her hand, and she said, "Up with you now, little lazybones, Maria's already gone to school. And don't you remember, they're stripping the pear tree today? You'll have to hurry if you want to get some!"

Martin's mother had blue eyes and brown hair; and in those days these eyes were still smiling and bright.

She laid the shirt on the bed and nodded to him and went out.

Maria was Martin's big sister. She was nine years old. She already went to school and already knew the names of lots of things in French.

But Martin still had sleep in his eyes and the swirling confusion of the dream in his head and couldn't bring himself to rise.

The blinds had been drawn up and the sun shone straight into the room. The door to the kitchen stood ajar. Lotta was lying at the kitchen window and talking to someone; no doubt it was Häggbom, the doorman. Eventually Häggbom started to sing, down in the yard, in his boozy voice:

"If I was rich as Solomon
And had such money to burn,
I'd be off to the land of the Ottoman
And buy me a hundred girls."

"And what would you do with a hundred girls?" asked Lotta. "Mr Häggbom, who can't even see to his old lady once?"

Martin couldn't hear Häggbom's reply, but Lotta started to roar with laughter.

"You've no shame at all," she said.

Now Martin guessed the doorman's wife had come out into the yard: it sounded as if she was pouring out a tub of dirty dishwater. Then she started remonstrating with Häggbom, and with Lotta too. But Lotta just laughed and slammed the window.

Martin lay half awake staring at the cracks in the ceiling. One of them was just like Mistress Häggbom, if you looked at it the right way.

The Ladugårdsland church clock struck nine, and when it had finished striking the clock in the hall began. Martin jumped out of bed and ran to the window to see if there were any pears left on the tree.

The pear tree in the yard was dear to all the cats and all the children in the building. It was big and old, and many of its boughs were already withered and dead; but the others still bore flowers and leaves every spring and fruit every autumn.

Häggbom's boys were sitting atop the tree throwing down

pears, having first filled their own pockets, and down below the rest of the children were squabbling over every pear that fell. In the middle of the pack stood Mrs Lundgren, wide and loud, striving to ensure that justice was done; but nobody took any notice of her. Some way off stood little Ida Dupont, wide-eyed, with her hands behind her back; she dared not venture into the fray. And Mrs Lundgren did not get her a pear, because she'd fallen out with Mr Dupont, who was a cellist in the orchestra of the Royal Opera.

Martin grew excited, threw on his clothes in great haste and came down the stairs.

Lotta yelled after him: "Aren't you going to get washed and comb your hair first?"

But Martin was already in the yard. Mrs Lundgren at once took him under her wing.

"Throw down a pear for Martin, John . . . Now, hold out your cap, little one, and then you'll get a pear —"

A pear duly appeared in the cap. But now Martin couldn't find his penknife: he wanted to peel the pear.

"Give me the pear and I'll peel it for you," said Mrs Lundgren.

And she took the pear and bit into it with her big yellow teeth and ripped off a piece of skin. Martin's eyes gaped and he flushed bright red. He absolutely did not want a pear at all now.

Mr Dupont was lounging at his window in his shirtsleeves with a red calotte on his head and smoking a pipe. Now he leaned forward and laughed at Mrs Lundgren.

Mrs Lundgren grew cross. "He's a spoiled child," she said.

John triumphantly held the last pear aloft, and the children cheered and yelled, but he stuffed it into his trouser pocket. But then Billy found another one, which really was the very last. He caught sight of Ida Dupont standing off by the wall with tears in her eyes, and so he nobly threw the pear down into her pinafore. And the children cheered again: the pear tree had been stripped!

But now Mistress Häggbom came out: "Good God in heaven what a row! And my husband at death's door! Down from that tree, scallywags!"

A little while ago Häggbom had indeed lain ill, and his wife's imagination often reverted to that comparatively happy time.

The boys had come down from the tree; she grabbed John by the hair and Billy by the ear, and was about to drag them off; but Mrs Lundgren felt a little riled: for of course she had, in a sense, presided over this impugned affray. Besides, she enjoyed a good set-to, and she therefore did not omit to remonstrate rather sharply with Mistress Häggbom about all that was deficient in her conduct. The lady released her boys, the better to stand with arms akimbo, and a grand quarrel ensued. Spectators streamed in, and all over the gables every kitchen window was flung open.

Finally a voice cut through the row.

"Hush! The deputy director!"

It went completely quiet. Deputy Director Oldthusen had the biggest flat and was the building's most distinguished tenant. He was wearing a long, snug-fitting frock coat, and under his arm he carried a worn leather briefcase. Having descended the stairs he stopped and took a pinch of snuff. Then he walked slowly out through the doorway with the concerned, distracted air of a statesman.

Martin and Ida crept out onto the street, hand in hand. They ventured a few steps beyond the doorway; then they stopped in the middle of the street, squinting at the sun.

The street was bounded by wooden houses and slate roofs and green trees. The building where Martin lived was the only large stone building in the entire street. The Long Terrace opposite lay in shadow: a low-built, dirty grey terrace. Only really poor folk lived there, Martin's mother said. Only the rabble, said Mrs Lundgren. In the dye works a little further down the street all was quiet. The dyer was standing in his doorway in his slippers and white linen coat and talking to the lady from the shop. It was even quiet outside the pub on the corner. A builder's cart was stopped outside; the horse stood with forelegs bound, eating oats from a nosebag.

The Ladugårdsland church clock struck ten.

Ida pointed down the street: "Here comes the goat lady."

The goat lady was approaching with both her goats. One she led on a rope, the other walked free. The deputy director's little granddaughter had whooping cough and drank goat's milk.

"Yes, and there's the rag-and-bone man."

The rag-and-bone man stooped into the courtyard with his sack on his back and his mottled black stick. People said he'd seen better days.

Two drunks came out of the pub and reeled down the road, arm in arm. A police constable in white linen trousers strode back and forth; a copy of *The Fatherland* was sticking out of his back pocket. A flock of chickens processed out of the courtyard at the Long Terrace, the cockerel at its head; the policeman stopped, produced half a bread roll from a back pocket, and began to feed them.

"What shall we do?" asked Ida.

"I don't know," said Martin.

He looked quite helpless.

"Do you want my pear?"

Ida got the pear out of her pocket and held it under Martin's nose. It looked very tempting.

"We can share it," suggested Martin.

"Yes, of course we can."

"But I don't have a knife to cut it with . . ."

"That doesn't matter. You bite in first, then I'll bite."

Martin bit, and Ida bit. Martin forgot that he wanted the pear peeled.

Now there was someone calling for Martin, and the next moment grandmother came out and took him by the hand.

"What in heaven's name are you thinking of today? Aren't you going to comb your hair and get washed and eat breakfast? The devil'll take such a boy as you!"

Grandmother meant a severe reproach, but Martin just laughed.

In the gateway they met Häggbom; he was already walking a little unsteadily. He stood aside with a broad veer and took off his cap very politely while slurring away at his song:

"I'd be off to the land of the Ottoman
And buy me a hundred girls."

In the yard all was quiet now. Mistress Häggbom's fat ginger cat lay on the dustbin and purred with eyes half closed, and down below the rats scuttled in and out.

## 3

One grey October morning Martin got his mother's permission to go down to Ida Dupont's and play.

Mr Dupont's flat consisted of two small rooms on the first floor. At this hour he was off at rehearsals; Martin and Ida were alone.

It was a gloomy and cloudy day. The inner room lay in semi-darkness, tall wooden blinds before the window. Pulling aside the blinds a little, you could glimpse the big black dome of Ladugårdsland church between two grey buildings. *Ding-*

*dong*, went the bells.

Ida showed Martin a peep box with colour pictures. There were white palaces and gardens with long gleaming rows of coloured lights, yellow and red and blue. There were foreign cities with churches and bridges and steamboats and big ships on a broad river. And there were festively lit grand halls with blazing chandeliers, but the things that looked like flames were just little holes, punched out with pins. And everything in the peep box seemed large as life and indeed alive: it almost seemed to move, it was surely some sort of magic . . .

"I got it from my mum," explained Ida.

"But where is your mum?"

"She's away."

Martin looked baffled.

"What do you mean, away?"

"She went off with some gentleman. But sometimes she writes me letters which dad reads out to me; and sometimes I get beautiful things from her, things she sends me."

Martin grew very curious. He was keen to know more, but wasn't really sure if he should ask.

But Ida put her hands on Martin's shoulders and looked very serious: "Do you know what we're going to do now?" she asked. "We're going to dress up."

She pulled open a drawer and began to pick out red velvet bodices, silk twill and strips of corduroy with endless braids and rosettes; silk shoes, gloves and silk stockings and long lacy veils in pink, white and blue.

"I got these from my mother too . . . when she was with the ballet."

She took a sheer pale-blue veil with silver sequins and wrapped it round Martin's head. Then he acquired a red bodice, a sash of silver-shot gossamer, and a white skirt.

"You look so funny," said Ida. "Just like a girl!"

Martin looked at himself in the mirror and they both

laughed.

"Come here," said Ida, "and I'll draw a moustache on you."

Martin didn't think a moustache fitting, seeing as he was meant to be a girl. Ida had no such concerns: she charred a cork in a candle flame and drew a big black moustache on Martin, and she took the opportunity to blacken her eyebrows; then they looked in the mirror again and laughed.

"It's so beautiful, having black eyebrows," said Ida. "Don't you think I'm beautiful?"

"I do," said Martin.

Ida was a fount of ideas.

"If you want to be really nice, Martin, you'll have a party with me."

She went to a cabinet and found a half-empty wine bottle and a pair of green glasses. Then she put them on the dressing table and poured out the wine.

Martin was agog.

"Your dad lets you do that?"

"Of course. My dad lets me do whatever I want. My dad's nice. Is your dad nice?"

"Yes," replied Martin.

And they toasted and drank. It was a sweet, pleasant-tasting wine, and it glistened so gaily and so deeply red in the green glasses.

Outside it had started to snow: big, heavy flakes. The window ledge was completely white already. It was the first snow of winter; and the bells were ringing in the black church: *Ding-dong, ding-dong.* Martin and Ida knelt on a chair with arms around each other's necks and noses pressed against the pane.

Then Ida poured out some more wine and toasted with Martin again; and then she took an old violin down off the wall and started playing it, and as she played she danced too and waved a white veil. It sounded very odd when Ida played the violin. Martin stopped his ears and laughed and sang and screamed. But then Martin's back started to itch, and he remembered what his mum had said, that Ida Dupont had fleas.

\*

Martin was in the alcove by the bed, peering into the gloom. Farthest in was a picture of a Madonna behind two half-burned candles, and at its base hung a crucifix.

Martin stared in amazement.

"What is that?" he asked.

Ida became very grave and answered quietly, almost in a whisper: "That's our religion."

Mr Dupont was Catholic.

"Wait," said Ida, "sit there and be quiet, and I'll teach you our religion."

Ida wrapped herself in a pink lace with gold sequins. Then she walked forward and lit the candles under the Madonna: two still, clear flames. On a little shelf beneath the crucifix she lit some incense. The smoke curled out in blue clouds from beneath the alcove curtains, and the air grew heavy with a pungent, spicy scent.

The Madonna shone like an opera queen in red, blue and gold; and the stars on her gown sparkled and shimmered in the light from the candles.

Martin froze with delight.

But Ida fell to her knees before the Madonna. Her rich, deep-auburn pigtail gleamed like shiny copper in the candlelight. She muttered something Martin didn't understand, and her hands made peculiar gestures.

"What's that?" asked Martin. "Why are you doing that?"

"Hush! It's our religion."

And Ida carried on inside the alcove. Her big dark eyes

had a glittering sheen. But Martin felt strangely heavy in the head.

"Come here with me," said Ida. "Don't you think it's beautiful?"

Martin sat on the edge of the bed and tried to imitate Ida's gestures; but soon he started nodding . . . his head felt very heavy, so heavy . . .

Outside it was snowing still, and the church bells were ringing: *Ding-dong, ding-dong* . . .

When Mr Dupont came home the children lay asleep on the bed. The candles had burned out.


## 4


Autumn crept forth over the world, and in the city where Martin lived the houses stood grey and black with rain and smoke, and the days grew shorter.

But when afternoon came and dusk settled in, Martin Birck's father would often sit by the fire staring into the flames. He was no longer young. His clean-shaven face had angular, well-defined features, like an actor or a priest; and he had a certain way of smiling to himself without saying anything that inspired respect and a slight sense of unease. But when he smiled in this way his smile in fact in no way adverted to any failing or folly of his fellow man, for there was nothing of the satirical in his disposition; he was merely smiling at an anecdote he'd read in that morning's newspaper, or at a couple of dogs barking at the lions round Karl XIII's statue, which he'd seen when crossing the square on his way home from the ministry that afternoon: for Martin Birck's father was a civil servant. And although his salary was not large and he had no independent means, he knew how to arrange his affairs so that he and his family could lead a relatively trouble-free life: his tastes ran only to simple and innocent pleasures, and he was free from the vanity that might lead another man to try to mix with those who stood above him in wealth or rank.

He was the son of a craftsman, and when he came to consider his lot in life he did not compare himself with his more senior or wealthier colleagues but instead recalled the poor home from which he had come. And doing so he found himself to be happy, and had only the wish that no shadow should fall across the happiness he possessed. He was fond of his wife and his children, and loved nothing more in the world than his home. When he was away from his duties, he often worked with his hands. He repaired broken furniture, and he knew enough, though barely, to keep the old kitchen clock going, the one with a flower pattern on the face and big brass weights on the chain. He also made ingenious and entertaining toys for his children and pretty ornaments for his wife on her birthday. Among them was a little temple made of white cardboard. It was adorned with narrow gold bands, and behind a semicircle of slender columns was a mirror, which seemed to double their number. To the heights of the temple rose a spiral staircase, also made of cardboard and clad in marble-patterned paper, and the pinnacle itself was surrounded by a balustrade — also of marble. But within the staircase's lowest step was a little drawer that could be pulled out. And every year on her birthday Martin's mother would find a folded banknote or a little piece of jewellery in this drawer.

He loved music and singing too. He often sang *Gluntar* with an old student friend, Uncle Abraham, who sometimes came visiting; and he could improvise on the piano, and play tunes from his favourite operas by ear.

But he rarely read anything other than his newspaper.

Martin Birck's mother would often sit at the piano, with twilight setting in, and play and sing. Her voice sounded more beautiful than all other voices. She sang ballads nobody sang any more. Those were the times Martin and Maria stood behind her and listened, enchanted, and occasionally tried to sing along. There was a song about a soldier who'd kept a canteen from which he'd given a dying prince a drink on the battlefield: 'And the prince drank from it' — that was the refrain. And there was another song about a shepherdess who tended her flocks in a pass between two steep Alps, and then came the sound of an avalanche, and the girl hurried her flocks: 'Run, run, my lambs!' And as their mother sang her hands glided over the yellowed keys of the piano; the strings made a thin, glassy sound, and the pedals creaked and sighed; and in the bass there was a string broken and it buzzed from time to time.

It felt so desolate when she stopped singing.

Martin drifted here and there. It was as if the rooms grew larger and emptier as dusk fell.

Finally he turned to his grandmother, who was sitting by the window reading the *Svenska Dagbladet*.

"Please, grandma, tell me a story," said Martin.

But grandmother didn't know any new stories, and Martin had heard the old ones so many times already. Grandmother carried on reading the newspaper, glasses on the end of her nose.

"Good God in heaven," she suddenly said, and looked up over the paper, "did you know that a Miss Oldthusen's died?"

"Has she really?" said Martin's father. "Would she be a sister of the deputy director?"

"Heavens no, she was his aunt," said grandmother. "Her name was Pella: Pella Oldthusen. I remember her very well, I met her in Vaxholm many years ago. She was a terribly bright and entertaining old girl, but she was a kleptomaniac. Her friends would say: 'Don't leave anything lying round tonight, because Pella Oldthusen's coming over!' And she'd fostered a little girl, and when the time came for the girl to be got up for her first Communion, Miss Oldthusen stole her old maid's petticoats — they were hanging in the same wardrobe as her own clothes — and had them altered to fit the girl. Indeed, it's God's honest truth — I heard it myself from a woman who kept up very well with her and the whole family. Then the maid — who'd served her many years and knew her ways — said, 'Miss, miss, there's been thieves in the wardrobe! And more's the pity: they've stolen all my petticoats — though not yours, which were hanging right next to them.' — 'Can't think what the world's coming to, with rascals like that,' said Pella. 'It's terribly sad; but what can I do about it?' But a little while later she gave the maid money for new petticoats, because she was rich and not mean with it either; but the young girl got to go to the Lord's Holy Communion in the stolen petticoats."

Martin and Maria listened with mouths agape. So grandmother had told a story after all. And she knew many stories like it.

Father had lit a cigar and moved his chair closer to the fire. Then he beckoned Martin and Maria: "Come here, children, let's play."

The fire had almost burned out. Father broke up two or three matchboxes, and out of the pieces he constructed a building at the very front of the stove. He used a lot of matches too, as pillars and joists, and finally he twisted a piece of stiff card into a cone: that was a tower. Now he clipped off the apex of the cone to make a hole for the chimney. A stately palace arose, with colonnades and spires and towers, just like Stockholm's old palace in Dahlberg's *Svecia*. And when it was finished father set light to every corner.

It hissed and sparked and burned.

"Well just look — look how it burns! The fire's got to the

farthest corner . . . now the east wing's burning, and it's caving in . . . and the tower's burning . . . the tower's falling . . .

"And now it's done."

"Do it again, dad!" Martin pleaded, "Oh, do it again! Just once more!"

"No, not again," said father. "It's no fun the second time."

Martin begged and pleaded, but his father went over to the piano and stroked his wife's hair.

Martin sat down in front of the fire; it burned his cheeks but he couldn't tear himself away. It was blazing and glowing so dazzlingly there, deep within. It gleamed and glowed and burned.

Finally grandmother came and adjusted the damper and closed the flaps. Then Martin went over to the window.

The sun had long since set. The sky had cleared a little while ago, but still dark flocks of clouds drifted in straggling ranks across the pale glassy blue of the sky. The Long Terrace lay deep in darkness. The maples and cherry trees in the gardens had lost their leaves, and here and there a light from a window was already gleaming through the dark maze of branches. Down on the street a man was lighting the lamps; he was old and bent and wore a leather cap that almost covered his brow. Now he'd reached the lamp just opposite the window, on the other side of the street; once lit, the whole room brightened. The broken pattern of the white lace curtains appeared on the ceiling and the wall, and lilies, fuchsias and agapanthus painted fantastical shadows.

It grew ever darker.

You could see such a long way from up there — far over beyond the old, low-built quarter with its gardens and wooden houses. You could see Humlegården with the roof of the rotunda between the bare old lindens. And farthest off in the west a grey outline loomed: that was the observatory on its hill.

The deep empty blue of the October sky grew deeper and

emptier, and in the west the sky reddened, a red that seemed dirtied by soot and haze.

Martin drew pictures on the misting windowpane with his finger.

"Will it be Christmas soon, grandma?"

"Oh, a little while yet, my child . . ."

Martin stood for a long time with his nose pressed against the pane, staring at the sky, a gloomy twilight sky with pale red amongst grey clouds.

## 5

But once the lamp was lit and people were sitting around the circular table, each busy with their work, or a book or a newspaper, Martin went off and sat down in a corner, because he had suddenly become sad, without knowing why. There he sat in the dark, staring into the circle of yellow light within which the others sat together and worked or talked, and he felt excluded and abandoned and forgotten.

And it did not help when Maria found an old volume of *Near and Far* and showed him Garibaldi and the war in Poland and Emperor Napoleon with his pointy moustache; he'd seen them all before, many times. Nor did it help when she gave him a piece of paper and taught him how to fold it into a salt cellar, a crow and two boats joined together; because all Martin really wanted, without knowing it, was for someone to say or do something to make him cry. And so he sat sullen and silent, listening to the rain whipping against the window; because it had started to rain again, and the wind was shaking the windowpane.

"Yes," he suddenly heard his father saying to his mother,

"you may well be right, we should try to sell the piano and buy a upright instead, and pay by instalment. After all, it can't even hold its tuning for a fortnight; and an upright is a more attractive piece of furniture anyway."

Martin started at the words 'sell the piano'. He wasn't exactly sure what an upright was, but he didn't think it could be a proper piano; rather, he imagined something you wound up. And he didn't think any other instrument could sound as beautiful as their piano. Every bump and every scratch in the mahogany veneer was an old friend of his — he'd made most of them himself, after all — and he knew practically every key by the individual timbre of the sound it made. Sell the piano! To his ears it sounded inconceivable. It was almost as if he'd heard his parents calmly discussing selling grandmother and buying some old lady instead.

Martin started to cry before he knew it himself.

"Mum," said Maria, "Martin's crying!"

"Why are you crying, Martin?" asked mother.

Martin just sobbed.

"He's tired and sleepy," explained grandmother. "It's best if he goes to bed."

As Martin went tearfully round the company saying his goodnights, Lotta came in with the tea tray. It was with a very solemn air that she said, "I can report to the assembled company that Mr Häggbom is dead."

The room fell completely silent. Martin stopped crying.

Grandmother clasped her hands together.

"No! Is he really dead? That happened so suddenly . . . Good Lord, he's dead. Ah, yes, all that schnapps . . . But it was probably best for him, although it's going to be tight for Mistress H. now. He had his job as doorman, after all, and he provided for his wife and kids."

"He died at seven o'clock precisely," said Lotta.

But when nobody said anything she went out into the

kitchen again.

"It would probably be nice to send a note round the neighbours and get up a little collection," said mother.

Martin was sent to bed. His mother sat on the edge of the bed and said his prayers with him; he was let off with *God who holds the children dear* because he was so tired. After that he would normally have said *Our Father* and *Lord bless us* too.

Martin lay awake for a long time listening to the rain splashing on the window sill: he wasn't sleepy at all, he'd just said so to get out of reciting those long prayers that he didn't understand. Because it is quite impossible for a little child to associate any notion at all with expressions like 'hallowed be thy name' and 'thy kingdom come'. He lay thinking of Mr Häggbom and wondering if he'd go to heaven. He did always smell of booze, after all.

Martin was afraid of the dark. When Lotta came in with a candle to sort out something in the room, Martin asked her to leave it with him.

"You have to go to sleep," said Lotta, "otherwise Mr Häggbom will come and bite you!"

And she went out and took the candle with her.

Martin started crying again. The wind whistled in the cracks round the window, and now and then a door slammed, and somewhere outside a dog was howling. Before mother came and drew down the blinds, it seemed to Martin there was a red glow in the sky. Perhaps a fire had broken out in Söder . . .

There was a racket and rumpus down on the street: drunks turning out of the pubs, crashing and shouting . . . heavy footsteps on the cobbles, someone running and someone in pursuit, yelling, "Police! Police!"

Martin pulled the blanket over his head and cried himself to sleep.

# 6

The white winter arrived with sleigh bells and snow and ice flowers on the windowpanes. "Those are the dead flowers of summer come back to life," said Martin's mother. The spruce forests out in the country marched from darkness and isolation into the city's streets and squares, and when the Christmas bells rang in the holidays, a spruce tree stood in Martin's home too, dark and withdrawn and smelling of the forest, until evening came and it stood glittering with candles, white candles and coloured candles, and full of red winter apples, and sweets with little edifying messages on the wrappers that were so stupid even Martin and Maria could see how stupid they were. All the wonders of Christmas paraded by like the turning pages in a picture book, and when the star of New Year's Eve was shining above the white roofs and people said goodnight and gave thanks to one another for the year gone by, Martin contemplated with a shudder the string of grey winter days that lay before him and to which he could see no end; for it was such an impossibly long time till summer, and even longer till next Christmas. On New Year's Day he was woken to go out early, and it was still dark. Dizzy with sleep he crawled along through the snow at his parents' side, and when they turned the corner Ladugårdsland church stood before them like a huge lantern shining out over the white square, where people crept forth across the snow from every corner. Inside the church there was the boom of the organ and singing and lots of flickering candles, and Martin felt pleased and happy and thought that this was just the right way to begin the new year; and when the priest began his sermon he fell asleep at once. But when he woke up the pale glow of dawn was already lighting the windows in the dome, and his mother was shaking him and saying, "Now let's be off home for coffee."

And then everyone went home with hearts full of the most elevated intentions; for it was obvious to Martin that this was the kind of thing the priest had been talking about. And in the later part of the morning Martin and Maria were sent off on New Year visits, to Uncle Janne and Aunt Lovisa and to other aunts and uncles, and they were offered cakes and wine and sweets from the Christmas trees. But at Uncle Abraham's there was no Christmas tree, because he was a widower with no children and he lived on his own with his old housekeeper. Uncle Abraham was a doctor and many times he'd cured Martin and Maria of measles and scarlet fever and chest trouble. He had a black beard and a long crooked nose, for he was a Jew. And he had a parrot that could swear in French, and a black cat. This cat was called Kolmodin, and he was the cleverest cat in the world, because when he was outside the front door and wanted to be let in, he didn't miaow like other cats, but stood up on his hind legs, dug his claws into the bell rope and pulled very hard.

When, on this New Year's Day, Martin and Maria arrived to wish Uncle Abraham a happy New Year, he was sitting alone with a bottle of wine on the table and playing chess with himself.

The room was large and gloomy and full of books. Outside the snow was falling in big clumps. Uncle Abraham crammed their pockets full of sweets and got the parrot swearing in French and was very kind; but he didn't say much, and Kolmodin the cat sat in front of the flames glowing in the hearth and stared balefully at his master. Martin and Maria sat in silence and looked at one another and felt oppressed: for more than once they'd heard their parents say that Uncle Abraham was far from being a contented man, and that he never had been truly happy.

Thus was the new year begun. The almanac that Martin had given his father for Christmas had red covers, while the old one had blue. And to his surprise and disappointment Martin found that this was the only noticeable difference between the new year and the old: for the new days went by just like the old ones, with the ringing of bells, and snow and cloudy skies, with tedium over the old games and the old stories, and with longing to grow up. That was what he longed for, but he feared it too; because mother had so often pointed out the rag-and-bone man, the one who'd seen better days, and said that if Martin didn't eat up his gruel or his porridge, and if he wasn't a nice and diligent boy in every other way too, he'd become a rag-and-bone man just like that when he grew up. And when mother spoke this way his heart quailed and he saw himself creeping in through the courtyard door at dusk with a sack on his back and poking around in the dustbin with a black stick while his father, mother, sister and grandmother all sat gathered together round the lamp as before: because it never occurred to him to think that his home could ever break up and be dispersed.

Snow fell. A great deal of snow. The drifts grew and it turned sparkling cold. Martin had to stay indoors with his ABC and his times tables and his paint box and his marionettes and all the other already paling marvels that Christmas had left behind. But among the marionettes there was one, called the Red Turk, that he was fond of more than any other, because Uncle Abraham, who had given it to him, had said that it was the most peculiar marionette in the whole world.

"Look," he'd said one evening, "by itself there's nothing interesting or remarkable about a puppet that waves and kicks when you pull the strings. But the Red Turk is no ordinary puppet: he can think and feel just the way we do. And when you pull his strings and he starts to kick about, then he's saying to himself: 'I am a being with free will; I wave and kick about just as I please and entirely for my own amusement. Yay! There's nothing as much fun as waving and kicking about!' But when you stop pulling on the strings, then he starts to think he's tired and he says to himself: 'I don't give a fig about waving and kicking now; the best thing out is hanging stock-still on a peg on the wall.' So you see: he's the strangest puppet in the world!"

Martin didn't understand very much of this, but he grasped that the Red Turk was exceptional and held him in higher regard than before.

Thus the days passed, and on the twelfth day of Christmas the little family get-togethers began, when the Christmas trees were stripped and there were shadow plays and puppet shows and magic lanterns with colourful pictures on a ghostly white sheet. But on the way home the stars were twinkling and his father pointed to the sky and said, "That's the Milky Way, and that's the Big Dipper."

## 8

But one morning, when Martin woke up, he saw the sky shining a brighter blue than for a very long time, and water was dripping from the rooftops and the bare twigs of the pear tree. And as he sat upright in bed looking at this bright blue, Maria came in with a sprig that seemed to bloom in a hundred colours; but they weren't flowers but coloured feathers, and she smacked him with her sprig and danced and sang that it was Shrove Tuesday, and hooray, she had the day off school.

And there would be cream buns with marzipan inside for lunch.

And they took the feathers out of the sprig and wore them, and they played cowboys and Indians, except that they were both Indians.

But mother took the sprig and put it in the window in a jar full of water, in the sunlight — for the room faced east, towards the morning sun. And look: not many days went by before little brown-green buds appeared here and there on the twigs, and they swelled and grew larger, and one day they burst and were transformed into crumpled pale-green leaves, the whole sprig grew green, and now it was spring.

One afternoon a shaft of sunlight fell into the drawing room, which faced west.

"Look at the sun, children," said mother. "This is our first afternoon sunshine of the year."

The shaft of sun fell onto the pieces of the crystal chandelier, and it was shattered and spread rainbow-coloured flecks all around the room, on the furniture and the wallpaper. Father was just walking through the room; he set the triangular glass pieces in motion with a little swipe of his hand. The multicoloured flecks danced around the walls in whirry confusion, like a dance of fluttering butterflies. Martin and Maria started to chase them. They ran themselves red and hot and clapped their hands against the walls, and when they saw a fleck of sun outlined against their hands instead of the wallpaper, they cried in delight, "Now I've got him!"

But the very next second he slid away; slowly the ray of sunshine faded and the butterflies tired of fluttering and shining and were gone — Martin saw the last of them extinguished on his hand.

But no, it wasn't yet spring.

Again the snow fell, wet snow that melted at once and at once became dirty; again the bells rang in the black dome beneath a grey sky, and now it was Good Friday. Martin and Maria were in church, but they couldn't sit with their parents, because their parents were far off in the choir, in among a crowd of solemn people dressed in black; they were wearing black themselves, their father in evening dress with a white cravat; and everything was black: the red that once adorned the pulpit and the altar was gone, with black in its place; the priests wore black robes, a black cross loomed menacingly from the altarpiece's leaden clouds far off in the gloom of the chancel, and the low, dark-grey clouds outside stared in through the arch windows of the dome. Martin could not get to sleep as he normally did because everything was so dismal; the hymn wailed and lamented, the priest looked gloomy and mean and talked about blood, and a dog was howling out in the churchyard . . .

Martin was enchanted by all this, although he didn't know it.

No — spring, spring proper, that didn't come till the royal family drove out to Djurgården with a plumed and gold-trimmed team. How everything shone that day! How it gleamed of blue and sun and spring around the chimneys and rooftops, and around the weathervane atop the church spire! On Martin's street the maples were already in bloom, and above the crooked fences hung clouds of white blossom, cherry and hawthorn. The Square and Storgatan were teeming with people — the whole city had turned out in bright, colourful clothes, and before the Life Guard's barracks stood the pale-blue Life Guards themselves, whom Martin adored and admired, on sentry duty, sabres drawn. The royal family drove past in a cloud of plumes and gold, the people cheered and Martin cheered with them, and then everyone went out to Djurgården to drink fruit juice and water at Bellmansro. All around screeched violins and barrel organs and Martin felt completely happy.

But on the way home they stopped a moment to watch a Punch and Judy show. Dusk had already started to fall over the plain, but still people flocked together round the puppet theatre, where Punch was just in the process of beating his wife to death. Martin pressed in tight to his mother. In the half-light he saw the open-mouthed laughter all around; he understood nothing, but the sound of the wooden stick against the puppet's head scared him: were people really laughing at that wicked man over there beating his wife? Then came the Bailiff, and Punch beat him to death too; and he treated the Policeman and the Devil no better, until at last Death lured him down into his cauldron, and that was the end. Martin could neither laugh nor cry, he just stared in horrified amazement into this new world that was so unlike his own. On the way home he was tired and cold. The sun had set and it was getting darker and darker; the king had long since gone home to his palace, drunks jostled and bellowed all around. The white anemones Martin had picked on the edge of the wood had withered and he threw them away to be trampled in the muck.

But when at last they were home and it was night and Martin lay sleeping in his bed, he dreamed that father was beating mother over the head with a big stick.

9

Summer sky and summer sun, a white house among green trees . . .

In this white house Martin's parents had rented some low-ceilinged rooms with wobbly white furniture and the bluest blinds in the world for their little square windows. Just in front of these windows stretched a busy thoroughfare. Farmers' carts and wayfarers from the islands of Lake Mälaren were constantly passing by on the way to and from the city, and they all stopped here to pay their bridge tolls, because this white house was the bridge-keeper's house, and it lay just where the Nockeby bridge made land. And every evening the bridge-keeper sat in his porch, which was enveloped in hop vines, drinking his toddy and putting his cash box in the way of the travellers and talking and telling tall tales, because he'd been a captain on the high seas and travelled in many foreign lands. But now he was a little white-haired old man who'd had a lease on the bridge for years and was well off.

On the evening of the first day, while packing cases, trunks and clothes baskets stood higgledy-piggledy round the room, which still looked a little unfamiliar, though every cupboard and chair and every flower on the wallpaper seemed to say: soon we'll be familiar, and while supper, with butter and cheese and a few small cooked fish, awaited them on the table by the window, Martin was sitting in silence on the edge of a box and contemplating the strange new tableau: the grey roadway with the telegraph poles in which the wind sang, and the dark outlines of the horses and carts and country folk set against the blue-green western sky. But across the road, a little to one side, there was a hill with a clump of oak trees, their crowns standing weighty and majestic in the twilight of the summer evening; and among these oaks there was one that was black and bare, unable to grow green like the others, and in its boughs the crows had made their nest.

Martin couldn't take his eyes off this black tree with the crows' nest in its branches. He thought he knew this tree, that he'd seen it before or heard a tale about it.

And he dreamed about it at night.

Summer sky, summer days. Green meadows, green trees . . .

The meadows were full of flowers, and Martin and Maria picked them and bound them into bunches for their mother. And Maria said to Martin, "Watch out for the snakes! If you tread on a snake he thinks you did it on purpose, so he bites you." After that Martin trod as carefully as he could in the long grass. And she also taught him that it was a great pity to pick the white flowers of wild strawberries, because those were what the strawberries came from. And they agreed that the first to see a wild-strawberry flower should say: 'You go free!' And the one who said this would get to pick the berry of that flower when it was ripe. But when they reached the hill with the oak trees, everywhere beneath them was white with strawberry flowers; Maria was the first to see it, and at once she cried, "You all go free!" But when she saw that Martin didn't look entirely happy any more, she immediately suggested they share the treasure; and so they drew an imaginary line from one oak tree to another and thus divided the whole oak hill into two parts: to the right of the line was Maria's wild-strawberry patch, to the left, Martin's. Then they sat down in the shade of an oak and arranged their flowers as they liked them best; and Maria taught Martin to insert the delicate, heart-shaped quaking grass everywhere in amongst the oxeye daisies and the buttercups and to tie up the bouquet with long blades of grass. But Martin soon tired of his flowers, because he had forgotten that he'd picked them to give to his mother, and he left them lying in the grass and lay down on his back amidst them and looked at the clouds drifting across the blue sky far above his head. They were like white dogs, little shaggy white dogs. Perhaps they were little dogs. When people die, they go to heaven, of course; but dogs, which don't have proper souls, probably can't get up that high. But they can run around outside and play with one another; and sometimes their masters come out to them, and then the little dogs jump up and lick them and are so happy . . .

White clouds, summer clouds.

But best of all was the long bridge and the lake and all the steamboats, tooting for the bridge to open and let them through as they approached from far away. Martin soon learned to recognise them all: *Fyris* and *Garibaldi*, *Brage*, which was never in much of a hurry, the beautiful blue *Tynnelsö* and the brown *Enköping*, which they called the coffee percolator, because it chugged just like one. For Martin every boat had its own individual facial expression, so he could distinguish one from another a long way off. They helped him keep track of time too. When the *Tynnelsö* passed under the bridge it was time to go home and have lunch; and when the rasping whistle of *Runan* was heard you knew *Brage* wasn't far behind, and with *Brage* came dad from town. Then too there were tugboats pulling long rows of barges; these barges would often get stuck beneath the bridge, and nothing in the world was as much fun as hearing the men on the barges swearing. But on those days when the waters went green, with white foam and waves crashing high up over the bridge, no steamboat could compete with the little cargo boats from Roslag for pride of place in Martin's heart. In the captain of every little cargo boat Martin found a hero, defying wave and storm to reach some unknown, mysterious goal: because it never occurred to him that they were just sailing to Stockholm to sell the firewood or the hay or the clay pots they had onboard. Still, he found these things somehow disagreeable, because he couldn't help their instilling the dark suspicion of some tawdry ulterior motive on the part of the captain, and in the depths of his heart he liked best those cargo boats returning empty from the city. And those were the ones that danced most nimbly over the waves too, and headed off to places Martin had never been, far beyond Tyska Botten and Blackeberg, where the outermost limits of the known world ran.

That too was where the sun set every evening, in a red,

shimmering promised land. Martin was quite convinced that it was just there it set — right behind the promontory — and not in any other place; after all, he could see it happen, clear as could be. Nevertheless, he did not suppose that the people who lived over there got a really close look at the sun, or that they need live in fear of having it land on their heads. If some other lad had come up to him and suggested such things he'd have thought him pretty stupid. Because children, just like adults, regularly form the most peculiar notions about the world, but when someone teases out the consequences of their ideas they say that he's extremely stupid, or that you shouldn't make jokes about serious things.

Summertime, wild-strawberry time . . .

In those days summer was not the same as it is now. Summer was a happiness that filled the days and the evenings and permeated even your dreams at night; and morning was happiness itself. But one morning Martin woke earlier than usual, and when he heard a little bird twittering in the privet hedge outside the window and saw that the sun was shining, he sat up in bed and wanted to get dressed and go out. Then his mother came in and said that he should wait a little while, because it was his birthday, and Maria was busy with something out there that he wasn't to see until it was ready. And she kissed him and said that he was now seven years old and that he should be very diligent and well behaved this summer if he didn't want to feel ashamed of himself in front of the other boys in the autumn, when he'd be starting school.

But when Martin heard the word 'school' he forgot the bird that was twittering in the hedge, and the sun that was shining, and he felt his throat so choked, as if he was bound to cry; but he mastered himself and did not cry. He didn't know exactly what school meant, but the word sounded so nasty and harsh. It was true, indeed, that his mother conducted a 'school' with him and Maria, but that was just a little while each day down in the garden, in the lilac bower, where butterflies fluttered, yellow and white and blue ones, and the bumblebees buzzed, while his mother told him stories about Joseph in Egypt and about kings and prophets, and taught him to form letters from a template she'd made. And he grasped that a proper school must be something quite different. But just as Martin's heart was being seized with anxiety over the start of school in the autumn, everyone came in to wish him happy birthday, dad and grandmother and Maria, and Maria ostentatiously took centre stage and bowed and said, "I have the honour of wishing you many happy returns!" But Martin blushed and felt embarrassed and turned away to face the wall.

They left him alone. But it wasn't long before grandmother stuck her head round the door and called out that the king was coming riding with fifteen generals to wish Martin a happy birthday, and at that very moment you could hear a rumble over the bridge like thunder. Then he jumped out of bed and threw on his clothes, and the rumble came nearer, and there was a cloud of dust over the road, the horses' hooves thundered over the bridge and over the land, and swords and helmets flashed and shone. When he came out onto the veranda the frontmost riders were already long past, but Martin's mother consoled him that the king was not among them. The riders passing now were almost the whole of the king's cavalry, off to field manoeuvres at Drottningholm. There were hussars and dragoons and all the field artillery from Stockholm, and the artillerymen were being shaken like sacks of potatoes on their carts and were grey and black with dust and dirt. But Martin admired them even more like that, and contemplated whether it wasn't perhaps even better to be an artilleryman than the captain of a cargo boat.

But then the cavalry passed by and were gone, and a fresh wind blew in from the lake and brought with it the smell of muck and sweat that they'd left behind, and when Martin turned round there stood next to the breakfast table a specially small table laid just for him, and Maria had decked it with flowers and green leaves. Then once again Martin felt embarrassed and blushed, but he was also very happy, because in the middle of the table was a cake that his mother had baked for him, and a big plate full of wild strawberries, which Maria had picked from under the oaks, and a twenty-five öre piece from dad, and a parcel with socks that grandmother had knitted. But of all these Martin liked the twenty-five öre piece best: because he had already realised that a pair of socks is, well, a pair of socks, plain and simple, and a cake is a cake; but a twenty-five öre piece is an indefinite number of wishes fulfilled of any kind whatever, within a certain limit, and how confined a limit that was experience had not yet taught him.

And Martin went and thanked everyone and sampled the cake and the strawberries and saw that the socks had red stripes and looked really nice and tucked the twenty-five öre piece neatly away in a matchbox that he used as a cashbox, and where hitherto were just a few old coppers and some small stones that he'd picked out of the sand and kept, because they were so pretty.

Then came the whistle from *Brage* at Tyska Botten and father had to go to town; but Martin had the treat of an outing with mum and grandmother and Maria to Drottningholm. There the king's white summer palace lay, reflected in the brilliant waters of the cove, and the trees in the park were bigger than all others, and beneath them the shade was deep and cool. And over the dark waters of the ponds and the channels the swans glided forth with necks outstretched, and Martin couldn't believe they cared about anything else in the world but their own white dreams.

But grandmother had a French roll on her and she broke it into pieces and fed it to them the way you feed chickens.

Summer days, happy days, cornflowers blue amid the yellow rye . . .

Harvest time had almost arrived, and Martin was out walking with his mother; Maria, on her other side, now and then picked cornflowers out of the rye. Mother was wearing a pink dress and a straw hat with a wide brim and she was talking to them about people and the world and God.

"Look, Martin," she said, "there you have precisely the good ear and the thin ear we were reading about just the other day in the bower. Do you remember? The good ear bends right down to the earth because it has so many grains to bear; and you grind down the grains into flour in a mill, and you bake bread from the flour, and bread is good to eat when you're hungry. But the thin ear is of no use; the farmer throws it away or gives it to his horse to chew on, though it fattens the horse not at all. But still it rises up, so proud of its height, and looks down on all the other ears that stand bowed all around."

And his mother broke off the proud, thin ear and showed Martin that it was quite empty.

"Many people are like this too," she said. "You'll see that when you grow up; and you'll also see people hanging their heads to make others think they're among the good ears: but they're the very ones who are emptiest of all.

"But, my children, you're to remember that it's not for you to decide, not now and not when you're grown up, whether someone is one of the good ears or one of the thin ears. That is not a thing one man can ever really know about another. Only God knows that."

When his mother talked to Martin about God, he felt at once solemn and a bit embarrassed, rather like a little dog when you try to talk to him as if he were a person. Because when he heard his mother talking about the Garden of Eden and Noah's Ark he could perfectly well follow along, and see before his eyes the apple tree and the serpent and all the creatures in the Ark; but the word 'God' brought to mind no definite image, neither an old gent nor some middle-aged man with a dark beard. At the very highest point of the blue vault of Ladugårdsland church's dome there was a big painted eye, and mother had said it was a symbol of God. But that solitary eye struck Martin as such a woeful and eerie thing that he hardly dared look at it, and it didn't in the least help him understand what God actually looked like. He'd also had to learn the Ten Commandments by heart, which God had set down for Moses on Mount Sinai. But they only increased his secret suspicion that God was really a matter of concern only for grown-ups. It could hardly have been Martin that God was addressing when he said, 'Thou shalt have no other gods before me.' Martin neither knew what an idol looked like nor how one should go about worshiping it. As for honouring his parents, that was just obvious. Likewise he felt no inclination to kill or steal or covet his neighbour's maidservant, ox or donkey. And he had no idea at all how to go about committing adultery, but he resolved to be on his guard against it anyway, just to be on the safe side.

"God knows everything, that which happens now and that which will happen in the future. He himself has determined it all. And when you pray to God, Martin, don't imagine that with your prayers you'll make him alter his determination one iota. But God likes you to pray to him anyway, and therefore you should. You must never fail to recite your evening prayers every night before you go to sleep, no matter how old and wise you become. But when you grow up and you're making your own way in the world, never forget that first and foremost you must rely on yourself. God helps only those who help themselves. And should it ever happen that you so profoundly desire something that you think you could never be happy again without it — then you mustn't pray to God to give it to you. Rather, you must try to get it yourself; but if that can't be done, then pray to God to fortify you to do without what you desire. Those are the only prayers God likes."

Thus spoke Martin Birck's mother as they went on their way. And the summer wind whispered all around them, and it swept forth over the field, and the grain rippled.

\*

Now the bridge-keeper, the old man Moberg, had a boy by the name of Johan. Johan was fourteen or fifteen years old and soon became Martin's best friend. For Martin he carved archery bows and boats made from bark, and Martin helped him winch open the bridge. In the evenings, if he was free, he'd also play hide-and-seek or run the gauntlet with Martin and Maria and a few other children. But it wasn't because of the boats made of bark or the games that Martin was so fond of Johan and admired him so boundlessly. It was because Johan had such extraordinary tales to tell, tales about things mum and dad and grandmother never spoke of. It was especially towards evening that Johan became voluble, when he and Martin were sitting together on a beam by the drawbridge waiting for a steamboat that was due and whose lights would sooner or later emerge from behind the headland — first the green one, then the red. That was when Johan would talk about one thing and another. Now, it would be about old Moberg, who'd see tiny little devils jumping up and down, up and down in his toddy glass: and that was what he was talking about when he was sitting muttering to himself and swirling the toddy round in the glass. But with the priest in Lovön it was even worse: because, you see, he was on ever such good terms with the Devil, and the whole parish knew it. Though of course you could work it out for yourself if you thought about it: how else could anyone stand there in the pulpit and preach a whole hour long the way he did? Where did he get all the words from? In point of fact Johan himself had once run an errand to him and been in his room, and seen with his own eyes how it was chock full of books from top to bottom. No, no doubt at all he kept company with the Devil . . . Or, he'd talk about someone who'd been murdered on the road three years ago, very, very close by, and he described the place exactly: it was where, on one side, the forest was really dense, while on the opposite side there was a willow tree next to a telegraph pole. It was a cold November night it happened, and if you went past the place at the right time you could clearly hear moaning coming from the roadside ditch . . . But they never caught the one who did it.

When Martin heard stories like this he squeezed tight on Johan's arm, and he found his heart eased when the steamboat's lights came shining out of the dark and got closer, and when he heard the thunk-thunk of the engine and the commanding cry of the captain, and they had to hurry up and raise the bridge. And when they went home together over the bridge they were both fired up with thoughts of ghosts and murders and Johan said to Martin: "Listen! I think he's after us!"

Martin didn't know whether 'he' was the murderer or his victim, but he certainly thought he heard footsteps on the bridge and dared not turn round. But Johan, who had a sunny disposition, dissolved his fears by bursting into a cheerful song, and to the tune of *There sat an old man on Copenhagen Square* he sang:

"I walk towards death with every step I go,
Tillytillypompompo!"

And Martin began to join in and sing along.

But as they approached the bridge-keeper's house, Johan went quiet, and Martin sang alone at the top of his voice:

"I walk towards death with every step I go,

Tillytillypompompo!"

Now the bridge-keeper, old Moberg, was sitting in his vine-encrusted porch drinking toddy with two farmers by the light of a round Chinese lantern. And he was an old man and drank toddy every night, and people said he wasn't long for this earth; but he hated the thought of dying, and if he heard anyone talking about illness or death it was as if they were talking in obscenities — or something much worse, because obscenities could fall without offending his ears in the least, and indeed they rather perked him up. But when now he saw Martin coming along singing a funeral hymn to the tune of a cheeky street song, he got up and tottered a little way to meet him, and he stopped before him. Martin stopped too and fell silent at once and looked round for Johan, but Johan had vanished.

Old Moberg had gone blue in the face, and his voice was trembling when he said: "And you, you're supposed to be the child of a good family! I'll tell you, these are strange times we live in."

Then he went into his house without either drinking up his toddy or saying goodnight to the farmers, and he went to bed.

But Martin was left standing alone in the road, and all of a sudden it had gone so quiet around him. He could hear nothing but the sound of the farmers' canes, which they prodded hard against the ground as they walked off into the night without saying a word.

But Martin's parents had heard everything from the veranda at the side of the house.

"Come inside, Martin!"

Martin was as red as his shirt collar was white. Now he'd have to explain who'd taught him to sing like that. But he told them he'd made it up himself. His father explained to Martin how terribly badly he'd behaved, and Martin cried and was sent to bed. His mother cried too, when she said his prayers with him. She was shocked and upset: because the crimes of children are judged, like the crimes of adults, more according to the outrage they create than according to their own essential character. And Martin's transgression had created a frightful scene.

The most beautiful days of summer were past. Now the days were swept with wind and rain, and the lake waters were whipped up green; and at dusk the crows flapped round the oak-covered hillside with its bare oak tree.

When it rained, Martin read *The bee and the dove* and *What happened when the toad saw the bull*. And he also read *The little one goes to the city of dreams*:

> Ten little goldfish swim in a stream,
> Gliding around with no care.
> The little one goes to the city of dreams,
> The twilight will see him there.
> Now, soon
> Dreamers at night
> Sleep with expectant faces.
> Bright moon
> Sparkling lights
> Glimpsed in a thousand places.
> The launch is sailing, it's heading for land,
> Where happy folk gather and sing
> By lamps that run in a shimmering band,
> While bells in the city all ring.

The city. Martin got tears in his eyes. He'd often thought of the city lately and wondered whether everything was the same at home: because in winter Martin longed for the green grasses of summer and the wild strawberries in the forest; but once a string of summer days had passed and the greenery was no longer new, and the dandelions among the grasses turned grey with the dust of the road, then once more he'd dream of the glittering rows of street lights in the city, of Christmas and the snow and of grey twilights on a winter day before a lighted hearth.

10

The year turned full circle and it was autumn once again.

So much in town had changed. The Long Terrace, with its gardens and hovels, was gone; in its place a big brick building was rising into the sky, higher each day, blocking from sight both the lindens of Humlegården and the observatory on its hill. Everywhere the old was being torn down and the new built up, and every day from the heights and hills of Ladugårdslandet you could hear the boom of dynamite; except that Ladugårdslandet was called Östermalm now. And Mistress Häggbom was now to be Mrs Häggbom, and if anyone called her Mistress she replied, politely but firmly, "Keep up with the times!"

Martin started school, but it was a small, pleasant school and not nearly as bad as he'd imagined. It was just a matter of doing your homework, and then all went well. And Martin felt with pride his knowledge of the world expanding with every passing day: and every day the boundaries of time and space spread ever wider beneath his eyes; the world was much bigger than he'd dreamt, and so old that the mind went giddy before the number of years involved. And if you looked ahead, time knew no bounds at all, it just ran on into a dizzying blue eternity; but tracing backwards there was at least a beginning, be it ever so far off in the darkness, a point where you had to come to a halt: six thousand years before the birth of Our Saviour, God created the world. It said so, in so many words, in Martin's biblical history, on the first page.

And He'd done it in six days, although the teacher said the days were longer then.

But even if the days of Creation were perhaps a bit longer than regular weekdays, the case of Methuselah's nine hundred and sixty-nine years was quite different: at that time, you see, said the teacher, years didn't last as long as now.

There were so many new things to learn and understand, and in reality school held none of those terrors with which Martin had endowed it in his imagination.

But on the other hand the route to and from school was filled with all kinds of peril and intrigue. The malicious creatures they called louts, and who called Martin and his friends snobs, might be lying in wait round every street corner. The worst among these louts were the wild and dangerous louts from the Bog, who now and then would leave their murky abodes in the district between Humlegården and Roslagstorg — 'the Bog' — and take off in a raiding party; people said they used cudgels filled with lead shot. But more than these louts from the Bog, whom Martin had never seen and of whose existence he was not altogether convinced, he was afraid of the obnoxious lout Franz, who'd lived in the Long Terrace and who still lived on the same street: for this lout directed all his energies and all his ingenuity into making Martin's life a misery by day, and he pursued him all the way into his dreams at night.

But one day, when Martin was on his way home on his lunch break, he came across two of his schoolmates fighting with Franz on a street corner; and they'd already overpowered him and knocked him down and were pounding him with their fists. At about this time Martin had started reading books about cowboys and Indians, and at once he saw in Franz the model of a noble Red Indian and was eager not to miss such a propitious opportunity to win him over as a friend and ally against other louts. Thus he went forth and remonstrated with his schoolmates about how cowardly it was of them to fight two against one, how Franz lived on his street and was a fairly pleasant lout, and how they should leave him in peace. And while he drew the attention of his schoolmates like this, Franz managed to get to his feet and run away.

And so instead it was Martin who got the walloping intended for Franz. Not only that, he would long suffer his schoolmates' obloquy on account of his claim to be good friends with a lout. And the next time he met Franz on the street, outside the dyer's front door, Franz immediately tripped him up so he fell in the gutter, bloodied his nose with a punch, tore up his books, swore like a trooper and ran away.

Because he had not realised that he was meant to be a noble Red Indian. But then this Franz was no small-time lout like so many others, but an absolutely horrendous lout.


II


Martin moved on to secondary school.

There everything was so cold and alien. Grey walls, long corridors.

And the schoolyard was like the Sahara Desert. When the bell rang for his first break, Martin crept off to the lavatory to get away from his new classmates. But for the next they gathered round him in a circle and for a while stared at him in silence, till finally a small, broad-browed, ginger-haired boy opened his mouth to ask, "Who the hell are you?"

On hearing these words Martin dimly apprehended that something new in his life was now beginning. He'd been happy as a fish in the sea, like every child with kindly parents and a good home. Now the doors to a new world were opening — a completely new world, a world where he could no longer rely on the simple formula for getting by that his father and mother had taught him: be kindly and polite to everyone and never encroach on what belongs to others. What counted here was making swift and sure judgements about when to fight and when to run, and about when the circumstances permitted cunning and dissimulation to be used to good advantage. And it wasn't long before Martin found his way. He suddenly recalled numerous oaths and swearwords he'd heard from the bridge-keeper's lad in the country, and he lost no opportunity to deploy them in conversation with his peers when he thought it apposite. In this way his bond with them quickly strengthened, and in return they furnished him with much that was of value to a newcomer: which of the teachers were prone to clouting their charges, and which contented themselves with reprimands; that the worst of all was Master Sundell, who had mirrors in his spectacles and knew everything that was going on behind his back, and always wore rubber galoshes so as not to be heard approaching in the corridor; that Sausage Cake was nice, though he marked strictly, but that Flea was absolutely bloody useless.

12

And so year was laid upon year, and the new buried the old, while Martin slowly practised the two great arts of life, learning and forgetting. For like the gambler who, to endure until the last coin slips from his trembling hand, has to forget his losses for the profit that consumes him, so also for man, who cannot help but gamble, the art of forgetting is the greatest art, on which everything else depends.

And Martin forgot. The Red Turk, which had long since tired of kicking and waving, he forgot as completely as if it had never existed. And Uncle Abraham, who'd given it to him and who hanged himself with a curtain rope one rainy day when he no longer found life worth living, Martin soon forgot him too, if he did still turn up now and then in his dreams, a dark disquieting enigma. But as he forgot he learned too. One third of the truth was given to him by his teachers, another third brought by his classmates, who soon helped him lift the veil enveloping the Seventh Commandment and everything pertaining to it. Often they employed Holy Scripture to this end. They explained precisely what it was that Absalom did with his father's concubines on the roof of the palace, in front of all the people, and along with Ezekiel they revelled in Oholah's and Oholibah's abysmal sins. And if both these parts came mixed in with errors and lies, and if the third part of the truth, which perhaps was the most important and which it fell to Martin himself to seek out some day, was one that had not yet begun to preoccupy him, still every day that passed saw the widening of the rents experience had torn in the cobweb bushes of fairy tale and dream with which kindly hands had enclosed the little garden of his childhood, and ever more often, through their tatters, there gaped the vast, empty hole that people call the world.

# II

# The White Cap

*Translator's note: A white cap was gained on successfully completing secondary education.*

# I

When once Martin Birck had got his white cap, his first concern was to go into a tobacconist's and buy a walking cane and a packet of cigarettes. The girl in the shop had dark eyes and a bountiful fringe. Her appearance conformed only imperfectly to his oneiric ideal, which was blonder and owed something to Gretchen, but when she sweetly congratulated him on his white cap while regarding him with eyes full of kindness, irrespective of the fact that he'd never come into her shop before, he was suddenly so overcome with heartfelt warmth that he seized her somewhat grubby hand, which lay extended over the layers of Cameo and Duke of Durham on the counter, and tenderly kissed it. He nevertheless repented almost immediately of what he'd done. It was, perhaps, an indecorous act. Certainly he was under no illusion that this young girl was entirely innocent; no doubt she had a lover, or maybe several; but that didn't mean that just anyone could come in off the street and kiss her hand willy-nilly. He stood there embarrassed, not knowing what to say or do, till finally he pulled himself together, selected a cane, lit one of the cigarettes, paid and left.

Drottninggatan was still glistening wet after the last rain shower; little ladies with bouncing bustles raised their skirts to jump over the blue reflecting puddles; elegant gentlemen with narrow checked trouser legs and canes like Martin's waved their top hats in solemn greeting, thereby baring pates cropped so short the scalp shone through. Above the grey buildings' roofs and chimneys the restless white clouds of the spring day flowed swiftly past, and farthest down at the end of the street sunlight played round church and tower. Martin stopped in front of every other shop window to see his white cap reflected. He couldn't understand how he'd managed to pass. Right until the very end he'd thought he'd be failed. All the more pleasant, then, was his surprise when he received his certificate like the others, and especially when he came to the last lines: *Accordingly the said M. Birck has been found, in respect of the maturity that a completed elementary education is intended to confer, deserving of the classification: Pass with High Merit.* At these words his heart swelled with profound gratitude towards the teaching corps; for, while he certainly regarded himself as fairly mature, it far exceeded his expectations to find this estimate shared by his teachers. During the last terms he'd rarely done his homework. Often he hadn't even been able to bring himself to read through the assignments in the ten minute break before lessons began, or else sneak a few torn-out pages from the textbook into his Bible to study during morning prayer, while the religious education teacher stood spouting nonsense from the lectern, an expedient even the laziest of his classmates did not fail to employ. Nevertheless, even if he had no strong ambitions of his own in that direction, he would have heartily wished to please his parents with good grades. But in recent years a dull apathy had overcome him in all matters connected with school, and against this nothing was effective. He found it so difficult to take school properly seriously. If, exceptionally, he'd distinguished himself in one subject or another he'd almost feel ashamed of himself, as over some vulgarity. Whenever he delved down into the trivial details in which the textbooks so delighted he felt almost like the man whose house burns down, and who rescues the poker from the flames.

And now, with the poker well and truly rescued, he nevertheless felt so happy he wanted to sing; and he felt himself fortunate and free and hurried homewards with his white cap, home to the blossoming street of his childhood. But this street was no longer the same as before. From one solitary little patch of garden the cherry trees still spread their boughs out over a rickety fence — everything else was big red-brick buildings and tawdry little chapels. And the lout Franz could no longer disturb the peace of what little idyll remained, for he'd grown up and become an adult — yes, him too — and long since been sent to Långholmen jail.


## 2


Home was quieter and emptier now. Maria, Martin's sister had got married a year ago, to a doctor from a rural backwater, and grandmother was no more.

On this particular evening Martin and his friends were going to meet for dinner at the Hasselbacken. Martin's father gave him five kronas to spend on the pleasures of youth, and his mother took him aside and said, "Martin, you must promise me you'll be careful tonight and not get drawn into any mischief. Don't think you have to take a drink whenever someone toasts you, because if you do you'll get quite giddy. Best of all, just pretend to drink. And Martin, I have to tell you, there's a certain dreadful kind of woman who thinks of nothing but bringing young men to ruin. You must be especially wary of them. Oh, dearest Martin, if only I could be sure you followed the ways of God and were mindful of Him I wouldn't be worried for you; but of course I know you don't. Even the breath of these women is poison; just standing in the street talking to one you can catch the most appalling diseases, diseases no doctor in the whole world can cure."

"Mother dear," replied Martin, "in that you are quite mistaken." And he took his white cap and said farewell and left.

His mother followed him with troubled eyes, and when he was gone she sat down in a dark corner and cried: for she knew she would lose him, as mothers always lose their sons.

## 3

Martin thought about his mother as he walked down Storgatan on the way to Djurgården.

How could their relationship have become what it had become? To her he was still a little child. When he first started to speak to her about his religious doubts, she acted as if it was all something he'd got from somewhere else — from malevolent schoolmates or some infamous book. Since then it had got to the point where he could no longer talk to her about anything but the most mundane subjects — shirts and socks and buttons that needed sewing on. Should their conversations ever drift into weightier matters they would treat one another like small children, whereupon, without his meaning it or even noticing before it was too late, his voice would take on a haughtiness that wounded her, so that after such an exchange each would come away with a barb in their heart.

Often she would lie awake at night crying and grieving over his unbelief. And yet the whole of her being, and all her thoughts and all her hopes, were of this world. Certainly she believed in hell, because she believed in the Bible; but she could never in all seriousness imagine that her own son, or even for that matter any of those she knew and socialised with, could possibly end up in such a terrible place. And so it was not, in fact, for his immortal soul that she grieved, but for his future prospects here on earth: because she had observed that those who despised God and religion tended not to get on in the world. Some ended up in prison; some left the country to live among foreigners; all roused animosity and mistrust among respectable folk. She feared that this was the fate in store for her son, and it was this that kept her awake at night and made her eyes red with crying. She had no dearer wish than that he be 'like others', like people generally are, better and above all happier if possible, but fundamentally like them. She could well imagine her son becoming a poet — and she could even desire it, for she loved poetry, and it brought tears to her eyes when he read some of his poems to her; but if he did she still felt he should spend his weekdays as some official functionary and write verses only on Sundays or in some other spare time, verses about sunsets and the like, and send them to the Swedish Academy and win prizes and become at once a great poet and a respected official with a secure income. And she believed in all seriousness that he would be held in higher regard among poets if he had an official title and discharged his official duties than if he only wrote poems. Because that was how it had been with all the true poets. Tegnér, of course, was actually a bishop, and even Bellman had at least held an appointment at the National Lottery. And she would hold up to Martin as an example he ought especially to follow a poet she'd known in her youth, a man who was now a registrar at the Appeal Court and who wrote poems on beautiful and elevated themes, poems about the sun and the sea and the King, and who'd been awarded the Order of Vasa. A life such as that she felt noble and desirable, and when she entertained her loftiest aspirations for her son's future it was something of this sort she imagined.

But Martin dreamed different dreams. He wanted to be a *writer*. He'd write a book, a novel or a cycle of poems, or best of all a conceptual drama in the same metre as *Brand* or *Peer Gynt*. He'd devote his life to the pursuit of truth, and bestow on humanity whatever part of it he found or fancied himself to have found. And he'd also become famous and a Great Man and earn lots of money, and he'd buy a little house for his father and a new silk dress for his mother, because the old one was shabby and had generally seen far too much use. Men would envy him and women would desire him, but out of all the women in the world he'd love only one, and she'd be in love with someone else. This unhappy love would bring depth and bitterness to his thought and wings to his words. But Martin vaguely sensed that in seeking the truth he would find only truths, and while bestowing them on humanity in poetry more beautiful than any music, or in cold, clear, razor-sharp prose, he'd despise himself for reaping gold and honours from the trifles he chanced upon in the course of searching for something else; and this contempt would eat away at his soul and turn him into a hollow shell. But none of this would he allow the world to notice: he'd paint his cheeks with rouge and his eyes with ink and hold his head high, and at the very moment when he despised his own writing the most, and prized it less than the lowliest handicraft, mankind would be most captivated by it, and he'd be inducted into the Swedish Academy succeeding Wirsén. And with a face fixed as a mask he'd give the conventional laurel-strewn speech in praise of his predecessor. Never again would he set pen to paper. Living a remarkably colourful and tangled life he'd seek to deaden his despair. No vice would be unknown to him: in the light of day he'd drive through the streets in a cab with whores and buffoons, and he'd while the nights away with cards and booze, until, one gloomy evening in October, wearying of his wanton and empty life, he'd set a fire in the stove, burn up his papers and down a glass of dark-red wine, spiced with a strange special spice, and fall asleep never to wake again . . .

Or on second thoughts it might not be necessary for his life to end so tragically. Indeed, on closer examination it struck him as rather trite. He could of course readily move to a small town, to Strengnäs or Grenna. There he could rent a house and live alone with a parrot and a black cat. He could have an aquarium with goldfish too. He could dream away his days behind shuttered windows, but by night he'd light candles in every room and pace to and fro, back and forth and fret over all the world's vanity. And when the respectable city folk passed by his house on their way home from a night at the pub, they'd stop and point up at his windows and say, "There lives Martin Birck: he taught like a wise man and lived like a fool, and he's very unhappy."

These and many other things were the thoughts of Martin Birck as he walked down Storgatan and over Djurgården on the way to Hasselbacken.


# 4


The orchestra intoned the first bars of *Mefistofele*.

Martin was sitting outside with Henrik Rissler by the balcony rail. They were listening to the music and looking out over the terraces and not talking much. Henrik Rissler had a smooth, white brow and calm clear eyes. His gaze was long and inquiring and seemed to glide over the closest objects, the quicker to reach more distant ones. He was the only one of his classmates to seek Martin's company outside school. They would often go to one another's homes in the afternoons and chat and smoke cigarettes, and sometimes they'd go for long walks together, often in the rain or wind or snow, out towards Djurgården or Ladugårdsgärdet, talking about all those thing that preoccupy young men: about girls and God and the immortality of the soul. Or they'd walk through the gaslit streets with a feeling of casting themselves into the world's throng, stopping in front of the copperplate engravings in book sellers' windows; more than any other they admired a lithograph entitled *Don Juan aux Enfers* with a legend from Baudelaire:

Mais le calme héros, courbé sur sa rapière,
regardait le sillage et ne daignait rien voir.

This scene captured their imaginations, and their hearts raced faster whenever afterwards they brushed against a beautiful girl's arm in the city crowds, and every warm glance from a painted old barmaid they experienced as a love affair.

But the first ground of their friendship was that they both had read *Niels Lyhne* and adored it more than any other book.

Inside the restaurant people were talking and laughing around the punch bowls, gathering into coteries and cliques. Most formed, as by ancient custom, according to social and intellectual affinities and distinctions, which even at the school desks had brought together some and divided them from others: Gabel and Billfelt, Jansson and Moberg, Planius and Tullman. Others wandered around somewhat sullenly talking about unity and solidarity.

Josef Marin rapped on one bowl and called for a toast to the Ontological Argument. It was joined with relatively modest enthusiasm. The company was generally so weary of anything to do with school that they couldn't even be bothered to make fun of it.

Josef Marin was going to be a priest; but he was still not wholly secure in his faith.

The orchestra played student songs, *Stand fast* and *Sing of these happy days*. Twilight began to fall over the treetops, over the roofs and chimneys of the city and over the heights of the southern hills, the pale twilight of a spring evening that heightens and rarefies everything and renders it indistinct and dreamlike. The crowd, toasting and drinking down on the terrace, which just a little while before could clearly be resolved into its constituent parts, lieutenants and students, guardsmen and girls, and businessmen with their wives and children, now, in the dusk, had merged together into an undifferentiated mass; and, as if by an unaccountable whim, the hubbub suddenly quietened, so that for a second you could hear the splash of water in the fountain and the last sleepy tweetings of the birds in the trees. And in the west a solitary bright star was already shining.

"Look, Venus," said Henrik. "Look how she sparkles!"

Martin was sitting thinking, drawing on the table, and the lines he drew took the form of a woman's arms and breasts.

"Tell me," he suddenly asked, feeling himself blushing, "do you think it's possible for a man to live chastely until his true love comes along? Obviously that's how you'd want it to be. Going with women you feel nothing for, women who belong to another stock, foul mouthed with filthy clothes, thinking of nothing but their fee, that must be vile."

Henrik Rissler blushed a little too.

"Possible, yes." he said. "Indeed for some it's no doubt possible indefinitely. People are so different. But I know myself well enough already to see that it's scarcely possible for me. At the very least, the love of my life had better not keep me waiting too long . . ."

They sat in silence, staring at the star, sparkling ever more brilliantly in the deepening blue.

"Venus," muttered Martin, "Venus. A great and beautiful star. But I see no point in her having a name. At any rate, she doesn't come if you call her."

Suddenly Martin heard an unfamiliar voice behind his chair.

"Very true," said the voice, "very true! She doesn't come if you call her. An observation melancholy as it is apposite!"

Martin turned round, surprised. The stranger was a carelessly dressed man wearing a student cap, with a pale, narrow face and a black moustache that hung down over his mouth so that it was hard to tell whether he was smiling or in earnest. His face seemed a little old for the student cap, which in any case was not entirely clean.

One of Martin's fellow students was on hand to introduce him: Dr Markel.

Dr Markel had turned up in the company of one of Billfelt's older brothers. They'd arrived from Uppsala that very day, taken lunch at Hasselbacken and then invited themselves to the student party in the evening. Inside the restaurant the elder Billfelt was in the middle of a speech — Martin caught the words 'Uppsala' and 'alma mater'.

Without further ado Dr Markel sat down at Martin and Henrik's table.

"Two young poets, I presume?" he said. "I'm emboldened to presume, as I see you gentlemen sitting here by yourselves apart from the profane masses and holding forth about stars . . . Dare I enquire after your philosophy of life? Do you believe in God?"

Henrik Rissler regarded the stranger with some astonishment, and Martin shook his head.

Dr Markel appeared entirely serious; there was just a faint misting in his eyes, which were large and sorrowful.

Some of the others had come over to listen to the conversation. Planius and Tullman both put on the same scholarly face with which they habitually attended their teachers' explanations in school. Gabel's refined nobleman's face was smiling sarcastically, and Josef Marin pressed forth from behind him. Josef Marin was short and of slender build and looked pale and overtired. The two or three glasses of punch he'd drunk had already rendered him a little tipsy; but now, hearing a serious question and finding no mocking undertone in it, he said, with all the gravity he could muster at such short notice, "I believe in God. But I do not conceive of him as a personal being."

Dr Markel seemed pleasantly surprised.

"Ah, a pantheist, lovely!" he said, and turning to Martin added, "And you must become one too, I think, a man who means to be a poet. Yes, for a poet and indeed for anyone who wants to get girls into bed — as all poets do — I can't recommend the pantheistic worldview highly enough. Nothing could be better suited to turning a young lady's head than the pantheistic drivel with which Faust answered Gretchen's simple question, 'Do you believe in God?' If he'd answered as simply and unpretentiously as he was asked, 'No my child, I do not believe in God,' then to be sure the girl would have crossed herself and dashed into her room, *ins stille Kämmerlein*, and turned the key in the lock as far as it would go. Instead he answers that he both believes and does not believe, thus giving an impression of profound spiritual conflict, and hinting that God is actually the name of the feeling two lovers experience when they lie together in the same bed. He says this with great pathos and beautiful words so as not to wound her modesty: quite the contrary, she perceives him to be talking like a priest, and the rest is history. And for a poet . . . But first, as the senior student, permit me to . . ."

And with the insouciance of a worldly man Dr Markel proposed a move to first-name terms for all those who then happened to be within earshot, so they could all indulge in a fraternal toast; and then he continued: "For a poet pantheism is a real treasure, a veritable goldmine. A poet whose beliefs accord with the established church's will no doubt be awarded the Order of Karl XIII and make good money, but only prim little old ladies will ever read him and he'll be ridiculed in all the liberal newspapers, which of course are the ones with the biggest readership. An atheist, on the other hand, will be seen as a shallow and superficial character and a nasty human being and will find it hard to get credit. No, a poet ought to believe in God, but in a god who's something quite exceptional, *noch nie dagewesenes* — never before seen in public — and something you can never quite pin down, because of course then the game would at once be up. The god of the pantheist is precisely the raw material required for such a contrivance. For a god it's just perfect. Each and every one of us can tailor him to suit his own tastes; he never gets grumpy, and nor, of course, does he punish or reward, he takes everything in his stride, and all this because he lacks a little quality that subsists to a certain extent even in the most simple-minded of the yobs on Stadsgården quay: personality. And precisely this is his greatest merit: to a personal god one must stand in a personal relationship, which is to say a pietistic one. A splendid thing, indeed, for someone who's just been released from Långholmen jail and needs rehabilitating, but otherwise unnecessary. You can see what I'm getting at, gentlemen: adhering to a personal god entails a world of needless bother; doing without one altogether is too risky. Thus one needs an impersonal god. Such a god fires the imagination and lends itself well to poetry without imposing any duties in exchange. With such a god all educated people will regard you as an enlightened and right-thinking person, and you can become pretty much anything you want, from an archbishop to a radical newspaper editor.

"In a formal register he's referred to as the World Father, but in everyday speech, Our Lord. In point of fact he doesn't need a name — I mean, what's true of that star up there is true of him too: he doesn't come if you call."

The gesture which Dr Markel directed at the star and which so to speak beckoned her to him met only a dark and cloudy sky, for vast clouds had rolled in and the star was gone, and it had grown gloomy as on an autumn evening, and a few large raindrops had already begun to fall against the awning.

Dr Markel's performance was not well received. Josef Marin, who had had even more to drink in the meantime and

62

grown paler still, muttered something to the effect that he needed his face punching. Others stood around in groups and talked about leaving.

Sensing the mood, Billfelt senior rang for the waiter and ordered champagne. He raised his glass and, with beautifully rounded phrases, gave thanks for the kindness with which he and his friend Dr Markel, representatives of Uppsala and their alma mater, had been received by the soon-to-be alumni. Then he paid for the champagne and disappeared with Markel.

"Your brother is a true gentleman," said Gabel to Billfelt.

It rained as if the sky was open. The students crowded into a tram and headed to the city centre for coffee. Most favoured the Hamburger Börs.

Martin, who'd always been under the impression that the Hamburger Börs was the place where Stockholm's German businessmen met to do business, was surprised to find himself stepping into a restaurant that seemed to radiate a fabulous opulence. Here and there among the tables sat a few of his old teachers and a number of old family friends, raising their glasses and nodding agreeably.

Coffee and liqueurs arrived. Conversation turned to future plans. Most were set on a career in law and planned to spend summer studying for their preliminary legal exams. The atmosphere grew more buoyant, and thoughtless promises were exchanged to keep in touch, not to forget old acquaintances. At one end of the table Gabel and Billfelt were swearing eternal friendship, at the other Jansson sought to give expression to his sentiments towards Moberg. Only a considerable effort of will kept Josef Marin from prophesying. Josef Marin's prophesying consisted in reading out long strings of inconsequential information — wedding notices from *Dagens Nyheter* interspersed with extracts from Tegnér's poem *Svea* and Norbeck's *Theology* — all of which he recited in the same solemn, sing-song voice with which he imagined Elijah plagued Ahab and Ezekiel foretold the fall of Israel and Judah. The morning hour passed one and approached two, and a few of the party had already said goodnight and departed, in particular those who were quite serious about studying for their law exams. All around the clientele was thinning out, the electric lights had long since been turned off and only a few gas flames still burned, and the waiters stood around with martyred faces, longing for sleep and the contents of the tip jars. Nothing remained now but for the last of the group to leave.

Outside the sky had already started to brighten over the streets and squares; the rain had stopped, but the air still felt damp and cold and misty, and through the haze the clock face of St Jacob's Church shone like a moon from the *Fliegende Blätter*.

Still the schoolmates found it hard to break up, and they drifted along down Stråkvägen together, past the opera house. From its restaurant came poets and newspapermen, and Martin regarded them with reverence and wondered whether it would ever be given to him to be one of their number. The student caps shone white in the night, and like moths streetwalkers appeared from left and right, slipping their arms under the young men's and tempting them with promises of the highest joys life offered, and with cheerful chatter and innocent teases they all went down to Karl XII Square, because Josef Marin had got the idea that he had to prophesy to Karl XII himself. And as he delivered his prophecy Gabel took the prettiest girl by the waist and began to waltz round the statue with her, and Moberg followed his example and took to the floor with an aging bacchante, and Martin stood with pounding heart, staring at a small pale miserable girl with eyes black as coal, wondering whether he dare approach her, and as he wondered Planius put his arms round her waist and jostled her away, and Martin stood alone watching them twirling round in the mist, pair upon pair. But to the south of the city the morning breeze had started to clear the mists, and they drifted across the harbour like white smoke, and the cross atop Katarina Church's dome shone like the morning star in the first rays of the dawn.

A policeman came into view down on the quayside and slowly approached; one of the girls let out a little warning cry and the group scattered in all directions. A fat girl unceremoniously grabbed Martin by the arm and walked with him.

"I'm taking your arm, sweetheart," she said, "or else the copper'll have me. Though you're welcome to come home with me if you want. It's ever so nice there, you'll see. I've a lovely big bed, and I've embroidered the sheets myself. I do embroidery most mornings, you've got to have something to keep you busy, and I can't bear sitting playing *mariage* with Madam day in day out like those other girls, and they swear and carry on so. I don't like that sort of thing. I like nice kind boys like you best. And if you're really nice and come and see me a lot I'll embroider a nightshirt for you to remember me by. Oh, what, you've no money on you? Damn, well you can't then. But you can come again when you've got some. Just ask for Hulda. Look, is it really true there's a girl in Uppsala called Karl XII?"

"I don't know," replied Martin.

"Oh, well, bye then . . ."

It wasn't entirely true that Martin had no money; he still had a few kronas left from the fee he'd received for a poem he'd published in *Hemvännen*; he'd only said it so as not to hurt her feelings.

# 5

Martin lay awake for a long time and couldn't sleep. It was the pale little dark-haired girl who gave him no peace. She'd stood there so quiet and pale and alone. She'd taken no one's arm, and not laughed or chatted like the others. Who was she, and how had she come to be where she was? No doubt she'd been seduced and abandoned, and perhaps she had a little child who would starve and freeze unless she brought it food and clothes by selling her body. How he'd kiss her now, if he held her in his arms, how he would caress her and call her the tenderest names and try to bring her to forget who she was, a common streetwalker, and who he was, a casual paying customer like all the rest! Who was she with now, maybe Planius? What was Planius to her? He was no better looking than Martin, and he was dumb as a bag of hammers. He'd been one of the absolute worst swots at school and still only managed a *Pass* on his leaving certificate. Why should she choose him? But of course she wasn't making a choice at all: she'd taken the first to come to hand. Martin understood that and found it natural. Once, she'd given her heart and soul, and now she had nothing to give but her body — and why should she deny that to anyone when selling it was simply her profession, and when she'd already fallen as deep in the mire as anyone could? But perhaps, even so, if Martin could meet her and she got to know him, perhaps she might grow fond of him and start a new life. For her he would give up everything — all his dreams of literary honours, his whole future he would sacrifice for her: he'd settle for some job that would support them both straight away, they'd marry and live far from other people, in a little house by a lake deep in the forest. Together they'd row in a little boat in among the reeds and dream away the hours, they'd make land on an islet and there they'd be together the whole night long as the stars blazed above their heads. Every care and every dark memory he would kiss from her brow, and he would love her little child as if it were his own . . .

But while Martin was fantasising like this he knew perfectly well that beneath it all there lay nothing but desire, a young man's hunger for a woman's white body. And the longer the night wore on, as he lay awake staring at the grey dawn light creeping in behind the blinds, the more bitterly he regretted that he'd turned down the other one, the fat one.

# 6

When someone asks a young man, fresh out of school, what he wants to do with his life, he can hardly reply: become a writer. If he said that everyone would avert their eyes and a deafening silence would ensue. He might reply: become a lawyer, or a painter, or a musician, because he can train for all these vocations at appropriate higher education institutions, and even as he does so he has a little place in society, a certain status, a nook he can call his own: he already *is* something: a university student, or a pupil at a fine arts academy or a conservatory. It may not be much, but still it constitutes a little titbit to cast in the maw of the odiously inquisitive and importunate, and an at least somewhat comprehensible future to exhibit to the benevolent. But the man who wants to become a writer is nothing but a laughing stock for God and man alike — until he's renowned and celebrated. Therefore, during the long years of his apprenticeship, he must set a mendacious sign above his door and pretend to occupy himself with something people regard as worthwhile.

This Martin understood, and it seemed entirely natural to

him that it could not be otherwise; and when his father asked him what he wanted to do, he did not reply that he wanted to become a writer, but that he wanted to work as an assistant in the office of some government department. And his father took pleasure in this reply, seeing in it a sign that his son would be just as prudent and content as he himself. He'd harboured the fear that perhaps Martin might want to go to Uppsala and study aesthetics, and he'd felt that in that case he could not refuse, though he shuddered at the thought of all the worry and expense entailed in maintaining the son of a poor family at university. Thus he was delighted with the reply he now received, and could observe only that Martin ought to seek appointment not in a single department, but in as many as possible; and in the evening he invited Martin to accompany him to Blanch's restaurant to listen to music and drink toddy.

But on the very next day he was setting the wheels in motion and talking to his acquaintances in the various departments, and helping Martin write his applications.

# 7

But Martin was required to report in person to the head of the department on which he'd chiefly set his sights, and at eight o'clock in the morning and wearing a dress suit and a white cravat. Cold and hungry — he'd not had time to eat anything — he climbed the stairs of a quiet apartment block on an exclusive street and rang the bell of the director general's door. A servant in a gold-trimmed uniform announced him and opened the door to a gloomy dressing room with half-drawn blinds. All sorts of clothing lay strewn over the chairs, and the large green sash of an order of nobility was draped round a mirror on the dresser; by the threshold stood a chamber pot that Martin almost tripped over; but he checked himself in time and now stood in a silent bow. In the middle of the room was a venerable old man in a purple velvet dressing gown, gesticulating with a shaving knife, his chin covered in soap; and from the purple velvet and the white soap a voice rose and said, "Your examination results are excellent, but never forget that integrity and industry are and will remain the preeminent virtues in the service of the state. Your application has been accepted and you can report tomorrow to begin work, assuming there is any. Remember: honesty before everything. Farewell."

Martin assumed that this peremptory address merely accorded with established tradition and didn't allow himself to become alarmed. He duly arrived at the office, got a seat at a table and a thick ledger to scrutinise. He summed column after column. If the tallies agreed he was to put a tick in the margin; if they did not, he was to note the fact. But they always agreed. Slowly, Martin became convinced that there never were any errors in these accounts, and when once this conviction had taken hold he dispensed with the arithmetic altogether and just entered the ticks. And occasionally he looked up from his actual or apparent work and listened to the flies buzzing or the rain splashing on the window sill, or to the conversations and quarrels of his elders, or to a blind man playing the flute in the courtyard.

And he said to himself: So then, this is life.

# 8

But for Martin this was not life. For him it was a hiding place, an asylum in which he'd sought refuge for a time, a time he hoped he might make short.

He read and he thought. In books and in his own thoughts he sought what people so often seek in their youth, only to forget in old age that they ever troubled themselves about it: a belief to live by, a star to steer by, a coherence in the world, a meaning and a goal.

Martin had been a Christian until his sixteenth year. It's natural for a child to believe that what grown-ups say is true, and Martin had believed everything and doubted nothing, and on Sundays gone to church with his parents. If the priest were an eloquent charlatan, he'd feel moved and edified and would wish that he himself could be such a priest; but if he were a plain honest man, preaching as well as he could without any histrionics or theatrics, Martin would generally fall asleep. But as his sixteenth birthday approached he went to confirmation classes. Religion had hitherto been a mere detail in schoolwork, one sideline among others; now suddenly it became central, daily demanding time and thought; and nor was it content with thought: it laid claim to the emotions too, for it was quite usual to cry when actually being confirmed; and religion quite openly elaborated its claim to be the highest matter of all, the principal force in life, the only thing of ultimate importance. And Martin could not help but see that if religion were the truth, then all these claims were valid too, indeed, urgently compelling. In that case he would have to dedicate all his strength to it, his entire soul: he would become devout. But if it were not true, then he would have to seek the truth wherever he might find it — become a freethinker, in other words. The 'middle way' — the Christianity of everyday custom and habit, as professed and believed by the masses, that was for him unthinking and banal: it was an expedient that struck him as natural for the majority of his schoolmates, but he never saw it as a course open to him. He was standing before a fork in the road and he had to choose.

But one night, lying awake fretting over the question and unable to sleep, with the moon shining straight into his room and thoughts crowding into his head, it suddenly became quite clear to him that he did not believe. It suddenly seemed as if he'd long realised that the Christian religion was something nobody, in fact, could believe in if they wanted to be honest with themselves. It became obvious to him that the question of Christianity's veracity was something he'd already transcended, and that what was troubling him now was actually another question entirely: how could it be that the others could believe, but he could not? And by 'the others' he meant not only his classmates — because they never seemed to bother themselves very much about such things, and besides he knew perfectly well that they could be brought to believe in a little bit of everything — but his parents, his teachers and all the adults, who must know more about life and the world than he. How could it be that he, Martin Birck, still not sixteen years old, lying in a little iron bed in his parents' home, could think differently from the old and experienced about the highest and most important things, and that he could be right and they wrong? This seemed to him almost as great a lunacy as the very set of beliefs he'd just cast off. Here all his efforts came to a fruitless end, the puzzle unresolved. He rose from his bed and walked to the window. Snow shone white from the rooftops; the houses were all in darkness and the street was empty. The moon stood high in the heavens, but it was a grey-white winter moon, tiny and frozen and infinitely remote, and in the moonlit haze the stars twinkled lazily and pale. Martin stood drawing on the windowpane with his finger. "God, give me a sign," he whispered. And for a long time he stood at the window, staring at the moon and freezing, watching it slowly glide and hide itself behind a black factory chimney; and he watched it creeping out again on the other side. But he received no sign.

And nor, in the depths of his heart, did he want one, for he knew that a true conviction was something one neither could nor should be granted for nothing, by a miracle. Seeking the truth and, doing so, being honest with yourself: this was the only guiding principle he could distil.

Martin saw confirmation and attendance at his first Communion as duties, prescribed by law and thus unavoidable. His father knew no differently, or if he did he didn't say so, observing the principle that while talk is silver, silence is golden. And so Martin went to Communion with the others in his class. It was a spring day, sunny and with the first greening of the churchyard's old trees, and when Martin heard the church bells resounding and the organ took up the tune of the processional hymn, his eyes filled with tears and his heart grieved that he was not like the others and could not believe and feel as they did. And when he saw the church full of solemn people, and heard the voice of his teacher from the pulpit exhorting the young always to hold true to the faith of their fathers, he felt anxious and confused to the depths of his soul, and once again the same mystery tormented him: how can it be that they can all believe but not I? For of course it's madness to suppose that I alone can be right and they wrong — all the living, and the dead sleeping in the graves out there who lived and died in the faith I renounce. It's madness, insanity! I have to overcome my reason and learn to believe.

But when the ceremony itself arrived and he watched the priests in their capes moving back and forth before the altar as they attended to the bread and the wine and bore towels draped over their arms like waiters, his head swam with disgust and he could not believe that he'd ever been taken in by it. And although he knew — or believed — that these priests padding around in the dark over there were, in everyday life, pretty much as decent as people generally are, at that moment they struck him as utterly shameless frauds.

A belief in a god and in an afterlife was all that remained of his childhood faith; but his god was no longer a fatherly one who listened to prayers and nodded approvingly at them if they were good and reasonable or shook his head if they were childish and silly. Martin's god was ice cold and remote as the moon he'd stood staring at one winter night, and he stopped saying his evening prayers, because he no longer believed there was anyone to hear them. And at last the day came when Martin realised that the thing he'd lately been accustomed to calling god was not something a human being could enter into any kind of relationship with at all, not of love or obedience or of their opposites, and who could acquire the name 'god' only through a sloppy play on words and an abuse of the imperfections of language. And when next he scrutinised his belief in immortality he soon discovered that he had come a long way from the sky-blue kingdom of heaven of his childhood. He had noticed that everyone who defended belief in a life after this one on some basis other than revealed truth also presupposed a life before this one, and he found this natural and logical. The eternal is simply that which has always existed. Whatever at some time comes into existence will at some other time cease to exist: such was the law of all being. But Martin had no recollection of any prior existence, nor had he read or heard of anyone reporting such a thing with the least shred of credibility. Certainly there were people who claimed to remember past lives, but as a rule they maintained they'd been some famous figure whom they'd read about in books in the course of their present one: Julius Caesar or Pope Gregory VII. Only very rarely did someone recollect being a slave or a waiter or a shop assistant. This was a curious state of affairs. At any rate it was clear that the great majority of people, Martin included, had not the slightest memory of a previous existence. From this he inferred that in a future life he would likewise be unable to recall anything of his present one, indeed, that he wouldn't even be able to establish his own prior identity; and he considered that calling such an ongoing existence immortality was, again, as with god, merely slapdash thinking and a play on the imperfections of language and nothing more. And still more bizarre in his view was to give the name immortality to the dissolution and dispersion of a corpse into the natural world, into plants and animals and air and water. He'd little taste for such games with words.

Thus it was that Martin entered into adult life without any other faith than the belief that he would grow and age and die like a tree in the earth, like his father before him, and that the green earth which he saw with his own eyes was his only home among all the worlds and the only space in which it was given to him to live and act. And among the many dreams he wove round his life was the dream that he would become as a great and beautiful tree by the wayside, with a rich crown affording shade and shelter to many. He would create beauty and happiness around him and dispel delusions; and he'd speak and write in such a way that everyone must at once realise that he was right. He was, indeed, not wholly certain that the truth in and of itself made for happiness, but history had taught him that delusions made for misery and evil. The various religions had swept forth over the earth like plagues, and Martin was astounded when he contemplated all the destruction that had accompanied the progress of Christianity through different times and peoples. But he believed with perfect assurance that its days now were numbered. He seemed to sense that he was living at the dawn of a new era, and with his writing and his thinking he wanted to help clear a path for what was to come.

In the days when Martin's thoughts and beliefs ran like this, it still seemed to him that life, however short and perilous it might be, nevertheless had some sort of meaning. He felt himself to be in a process of development and growth, with new truths daily presenting in his thoughts and new beauties in his senses during his long solitary wanderings to the city outskirts or in the woods when the season turned to spring. And the spring . . . In those days spring was still a true spring — not an affliction, an intoxication, a fever in the blood in which all the old half-forgotten lacks and longings rise to the surface and say, 'Look, here I am! Do you recognise me? I've long been sleeping, but I'm not dead!' Not like that, but like a waking, a morning, a whisper in the air and a song resounding. And in those days the thousand unsatisfied longings he bore within him were as so many glittering hopes and half-spoken promises, for there were no long years of disappointment and emptiness to grind them to razor edges that cut and tear within the soul.

And however little he seriously believed that life would fulfil all these promises, or even the majority of them, they were nevertheless still present as compelling possibilities with which boundless, undirected dreams gained purchase; and even at the very moment when the book he was holding or the events of the day were whispering in his ear, warning him not to believe in happiness, they all fused together into a longing without bitterness and a wistfulness bright as a spring twilight.

And yet these warnings came ever more often, and ever more often, in the midst of those dreams his young blood bewitched him with, he found himself attending the other voice, the voice that rose up out of the depths of the most ancient times and echoed in the latest books of the day, the strange voice that none of the hundreds of new gospels whose words breeze through the minds of men regularly as storms in springtime has been able to silence for more than a moment, the voice that says: all is vanity, there's nothing new under the sun. What was he living for? What was the meaning of it all? He did not cease asking these questions, for he still longed to believe that beneath the life he saw before him there lay something else, something that could justly be called the meaning of life. For the greater part of the human happiness he saw around him, and the greater part of the happiness he saw men striving for, seemed to him like the fools' gold in the fairytale — actually nothing more than withered leaves; or else they seemed to him like amusing playthings, and nothing anyone could possibly take seriously. And whenever he turned his attention to his own life as he lived it from day to day, he could not escape the conclusion that it was in itself miserable and empty and that its only value lay in the uncertain hope that it would not always remain so. But what he hoped for was not something that could be approached step by step, with work and patience and a hundred little self-denials — prosperity and prestige and the like, that others had achieved before him — what Martin hoped for and waited on was something indefinite and ineffable; a sunrise, a thaw, an awakening from a distressing and meaningless dream.

Because it was as a distressing and confused dream that he perceived his life when he looked at it with eyes wide open and found it filled with paltry pleasures and commonplace sorrows and ignoble cares. Every now and then he would write some poems and short stories to earn a little money and test how far his words could follow his thoughts; but with each new year everything he had written in the course of the old came to seem childish and worthless, not amounting to anything that might fill him with creative pride. Beyond that he performed virtually automatically those deeds (or more properly, gestures) which would typically characterise a young man in government employ, or which circumstances might otherwise occasion. He went to his office as late in the day as possible and left it the moment propriety allowed. He made acquaintances among his colleagues at work and participated in their social events. He drank alcohol and dined out with friends in the evenings and paid money for cheap girls; he loved music and frequented the opera, sitting among the chimney sweeps and music enthusiasts in the fifth row, and he sang quartets and was inducted into Par Bricole, where an old headmaster hung the gilded tin horn round his neck on a rose-red ribbon with hands that bestowed a fatherly blessing.

And he said to himself: No, I'm dreaming. This is not life.

## 9

Years passed.

Martin was drifting around in the twilight. The streets and squares lay white, the snow falling soft and silent. A man walked in a zigzag ahead of him, lighting a gas lamp here, a gas lamp there.

Martin drifted aimlessly, scarcely knowing where he went.

Suddenly he noticed he was crying. He didn't really know why. Crying didn't normally come easily to him. Some snowflakes must have settled on his eyelashes and made his eyes wet . . . He turned into a side street and came to some parkland; he brushed by a couple half snowed-in on a bench and pressed on further, in among the trees where it was isolated and deserted and the branches drooped down under the wet snow.

. . . Strange. A hovel in an alleyway; a smouldering lamp. Two bare arms, bent, reaching forth by the window, the sound of blinds rolling down, and the girl, humming the latest song from the shows, slowly, indifferently undoing her red corset — he hummed along to avoid talking — was she pretty or ugly?

He didn't know; he'd barely looked at her; but it wasn't her he wanted.

He'd been sitting at home in the twilight, the icy blue twilight of a March afternoon, his mind tossing and turning over an old poem he could never really finish. And then all of a sudden he'd thought of a woman. He'd seen her that morning as he came from his office, and the sight was an instant intoxication. She was walking in the sunshine, and many men turned their heads as she went by; but she seemed not to notice or even have the least idea of it. She was very young, perhaps eighteen or twenty; she was dressed neither expensively nor poorly, but her bearing was easy and carefree and perhaps a little proud, and she went on her way slender and erect with her brown hair shining in the sun, occasionally smiling to herself. Martin followed her at a distance as she walked up Östermalm before finally disappearing through a doorway.

And now she'd reappeared before him at dusk as he sat in his rocking chair hunting after a rhyme, and she gave him no peace: he threw the pen aside and went out.

There was no sunlight any more, it was snowing. He reached the large grey building he'd seen her enter and walked up and down the pavement opposite, watching as the lights came on in windows here and there. Who was she? He recalled seeing her exchange greetings with a gentleman he knew. He went inside and up the staircase and read the names by the doors; finally he felt childish and foolish, turned up the collar of his coat and went back out into the snow. He took the arm of the first girl to give him a meaningful look and accompanied her home.

Now he was standing there in her bedroom, motionless and silent, watching her undress as she chatted and hummed. He scarcely asked himself whether she was beautiful: he knew only that she could be ever so much more beautiful without his desiring her more, uglier without his desiring her less. Her profession had marked her. She was still young, but it was obvious that she'd long since tired of picking and choosing her clients. With the same accustomed movements of her hands — the robust hands of a working woman — she'd unfasten that shabby corset for whoever asked: the lieutenant and the accountant, the Chief Justice and the waiter, making no distinction between them, except that perhaps in her heart of hearts she preferred the waiter as less haughty than the rest and better understanding her. Where did she come from? Maybe from some backyard with a privy and a rubbish bin, maybe from some hut in a forest — actually that seemed most likely, there was still a glimmer of the forest lake in her eyes. A happy girl among happy children she'd have run round the hills barefoot and picked wild strawberries. Early on her peers would have taught her to bite into forbidden fruit. Then she'd come to the city, and things had turned out the way they do for so many. Maybe it wasn't actually inevitable — she might perhaps have become the wife of a working man if she'd wanted, but in her eyes theirs was a harder lot and without too much thought she'd trodden the path that suited her best. With a little more brains and better luck she might even have become a middle-class housewife, strolling round the market square with her maid and haggling over the price of horseradish stew.

"Well," she said, "aren't you going to take off your clothes?"

He stared rigidly at her and suddenly was at a loss to understand any of it — why he'd come here, what he wanted with her. He mumbled something about not feeling well, put a few kronas on the commode and left. She didn't get angry, she just looked surprised; no taunts or jeers followed him down the stairs.

Still it was snowing. Would this winter never end? It was towards the end of March and still the trees were weighed down with snow and it was bitterly cold . . .

Martin was tired. He sat on a bench under one of the white trees and allowed the snow to settle deep on his hat and his shoulders.

What are we doing with our lives, we men and women?

At that moment the life he led, the meagre pleasure he sought and occasionally even found, struck him as a delusion from a madhouse. And yet this life of his was a normal one: most of the men he knew lived this way. He was twenty-three years old. He'd been playing this game for four or five years now, he ought to be used to it . . .

No, he didn't understand people — and he didn't understand himself either. He would often listen to his friends and acquaintances talking about these things. He'd noticed that most respectable young men, and old ones for that matter, believed in two kinds of love: a pure sort, and a carnal sort. Girls from good homes were to be loved with the pure sort, but that entailed betrothal and marriage for which the means were rarely to hand. As a rule, then, it was only wealthy girls who could inspire this pure love, it was otherwise an emotion that more properly belonged to lyric poetry than to reality. Carnal love, on the other hand, was something a normal young man could and should indulge in at least once a week; but this whole aspect of existence was regarded as having no serious significance — it wasn't something that could make a man happy or unhappy, it was mere comedy: the stuff of amusing stories and a recreation as agreeable as it was healthy when you'd drawn your salary and drunk a couple of pints. But the rest of the time few respectable and clean-living men concerned themselves with sex at all: they found its mechanics dirty and distasteful or, as they would put it themselves, beastly, because they could not perform them without feeling themselves to be beasts.

This view was the prevailing one everywhere in society

and, circumstances being as they were, such a way of living was proclaimed the healthiest and the wisest — not, to be sure, in priests' sermons or parliamentarians' speeches or the leading articles in the newspaper, but in enlightened opinion, man to man, in all circles. It was seen as a necessity, allowing young men to preserve their health and good humour, and girls from good homes their precious virtue. And the young men drank and frequented harlots and grew fat and rosy-cheeked and managed not merely to endure this life as a miserable proxy, but rather found it so appealing that often enough, even when married, they didn't despise an excursion to those old haunts that had grown so dear to them. And the girls from good homes, they got to retain their great virtue — admittedly without being consulted on the matter — though for some the weight of this precious jewel did at length become too great to bear . . .

What have we done with our lives, we men and women?

Happiness, the joy of youth — where did it lead? Life is attuned to the old: hence it is a misfortune to be young. It is attuned to the unthinking and the dull, to the ones who mistake the false for genuine, or even prefer what is false: that is why it is a sickness to think and to feel, a sickness of childhood, a thing one has to pass through before one becomes a man . . .

The shadow of a woman swept slowly by the bench where he sat and, scarcely past him, stopped. She turned her head and fixed her large dark eyes on him.

He got up, shook off the snow and left. He walked quickly: he was freezing.

He was thinking about life and about books. In his childhood a new kind of literature had appeared on the scene, taking issue with prevailing social morals and working to change them. Now it had fallen silent — yet so little had changed, practically nothing, and the matter had already been dropped. The things it'd been fighting for and for whose sake such cutting blows had been struck and received — suddenly that was just so 'eighties', and as such conclusively cross-examined and condemned once and for all, weighed in the balance and found — disturbingly plenteous. Instead, all around him, the blue flower of poetry was fragrant as never before. Once more the old words resounded as if new; the world grew young again, and again the forests and the waters were filled with centaurs and nymphs, knights and maidens joyously wandering beneath a setting sun, once more there was the goddess of song herself, eyes wide open, done with her long sleep, standing amid the people and singing as she hadn't sung in a hundred years. Martin loved this poetry — its words and rhythms crept into the verses he himself sat prodding into shape in the evenings — yet it was all peculiarly alien to him: the world was the same as before, everything still ran its familiar course, no victory had been won: was it really the time to be singing? It was indeed true that when he looked more closely he could probably discern certain ideas underlying these new poems too, ideas that themselves patently conflicted with prevailing norms; but only a few noticed this much, and hardly anyone attached any importance to it. They were just poems, after all.

They were poems, and as a forum for ideas they had been and remained on roughly the same level as the Royal Opera. There too the baritone could inveigh against tyranny without thereby compromising his chances of royal honours, there too seduction scenes were played out on heady oriental sets without anyone taking the least exception; what the bourgeoisie in their bourgeois lives regarded as beastly was, in *Faust* or in *Romeo and Juliet*, found by exactly the same people to be poetical and sweet and entirely suitable fare for teenage girls: and thus it was with poetry. Ideas wrapped up in verse and fine words were illicit no longer: they weren't even noticed.

If only someone would come along once again and not sing but speak, and speak clearly!

. . . He'd come out into Strandvägen. The ice in Nybro cove had just broken up; a tugboat was groaning its way between ice floes. To the left some newly built barracks for millionaires loomed up in the haze of snow; in one of them the electric lights and crystal chandeliers were already shining from a long suite of rooms, and in a grand ballroom a shimmering white mêlée of dancing couples swirled behind the muslin drapes.

A few lonely souls, wandering aimlessly, had stopped in a group and were staring up at that paradise as if nailed to the spot. Martin too stopped for a minute and then walked on in thought. A few bars of the waltz had found their way to his ears: *The Waves of the Danube*; he walked on humming it, unable to get it out of his head.

O Eros, Eros! The whore's bedchamber and that ballroom up there . . . it was the same god worshipped in both temples, and in both temples worshipped by the same men. But the women . . .

Martin didn't dance, but still he loved balls. He liked standing in doorways and watching the others whirling by. What was it about the mood at these young people's parties that so bewitched him and left him brooding, sick with longing for the impossible? Look at those women . . . held tight in the men's arms, eyes half shut, lips parted, the most innocent young girls swept by in dresses that revealed or showed off their heaving young breasts. What were they thinking about, what were they dreaming of? No doubt there were some without a thought in their heads, dreaming of trifles and desiring nothing but to move their legs and get a little exercise, proper young ladies after their mother's and aunties' own hearts. But probably not all were like that. The daughters of men could not have changed so terribly much from that none too distant time when lads and lasses carried images of phalluses in their processions and sang holy songs. What were they talking about, those girls, sitting in corners together whispering to one another? 'She's secretly engaged to him . . .', 'He's in love with her, but she likes somebody else . . .' The books they read: what are they about? They're about exactly the same things: about people in love with one another, and what happened then, and who got whom. 'Getting' — what does that mean? That you'll discover on your wedding night.

But the years pass and marriage — well perhaps that'll have to come when it does. The girl reaches twenty-five, she's getting on for thirty, and still she dances at balls with half-shut eyes, but her lips are no longer parted — she knows now that it looks unseemly and she keeps them tight shut, a blood-red strip. Will it never happen, this great and wonderful thing? She has the eyes of a drowning man: *Save me, I'm sinking, I'm going under! Youth is so fleeting — look at my skin, already growing pale, my bosom sagging, my young flower withering.* Now she tries being bold and provocative — she's afraid she's been too demure till now, perhaps it wasn't the best thing to do — but the gentlemen are already laughing behind her back, when toasting one another over the punchbowl, and a few deride her openly; others know her better — they can well imagine she'd make a good wife and an ardent lover — but they're not minded to marry, and as for seducing a girl from a good background, well, that's a dodgy undertaking when, leaving the ballroom, they can so easily, with so little fuss, just make their way to their old haunts, to the bedchamber with the smouldering lamp or with a red light of lust hanging from the ceiling.

What are we doing with our lives, we men — and what are we doing with *theirs*?

Martin turned back, in towards the centre of town.

On a street corner he met a poet, out walking and freezing in a thin yellow-green Ulster coat. He was a couple of years older than Martin and had already gained a little renown, writing as he did the loveliest verses on everything under the sun with the most tremendous facility — though mostly about girls and flowers and June nights on the plains of Scania, where he came from. He had a pallid face and a thin ginger beard, and whenever he met a fellow writer his big childlike eyes took on a wild, transfixed expression, as if he were weighing up the question: Shall I murder him, or shall we go somewhere and have a drink?

They went to the *Anglais* and had green chartreuse.

The poet talked about himself. He confided to Martin that he was a decadent. He adored everything that was in a state of decomposition and decay and doomed to extinction. He hated light and the sun — he shook his fist bitterly at the gas chandelier above them — he loved sin and the night and all the glittering green liqueurs. He had most of the known venereal diseases, and was agoraphobic too: no power on earth could make him cross Gustav Adolf Square on a diagonal. This illness gave him the most especial pleasure, because he thought it a harbinger of *paralysie générale*, and *paralysie générale* — that was the Great Sleep, that was Nirvana.

Martin listened distractedly. Light is good, he said to himself, and darkness is good too. But sometimes darkness is wicked, and light is wicked too . . .

"But how is it then," he asked, "that your poems differ in no significant respect from the ones that win prizes at the Academy?"

The poet's countenance darkened at these words; his lips suddenly grew thin and tight. He got a dirty flick knife out of his pocket, opened it halfway and put his index finger on the exposed blade.

"How long can you bear cold steel?" he asked.

"You quite misunderstand me," said Martin, and laid a calming hand on the poet's arm. "I love your poems. It's just that I don't see the connection between them and your own inner life as you've just described it . . ."

The poet smiled.

"It's amusing to hear you say you love my poems," he said. "You see, the ones I've published so far are just crap. But they'll do for the rabble. Look . . ."

And he produced a newspaper clipping from his pocket, a review of his latest volume, a famous name on the byline. The esteemed critic mildly lamented that some of the poems could not wholly be exonerated of intimating a certain sensualism, which was disagreeable; but elsewhere the poet adhered to purer tones, showing a rich promise for the future.

"Well, that's kind of him," Martin responded when he'd read it.

"Kind?" Once more the poet convulsively gripped the pocket with the knife. "Kind, you think? You don't think his sort should be crawling in the dirt before the most miserable poem of mine?"

"Yes," said Martin, "yes of course he should; but that's just not the way older people react to the young."

The poet fell silent, and drank, and remained silent for a long time.

Martin drank too. The strong green liquid burned in his palate and in his brain. And once more the woman was there, the one from that morning, walking in the sun and smiling. Perhaps she was smiling now, dreaming, smiling in her dreams? Or was she turning sleeplessly in her bed, longing for a man?

Perhaps he'd write to her. It wouldn't be hard to discover her name. No. She'd only show the letter to her girlfriends, and they'd laugh and giggle . . .

The restaurant was almost empty. Farthest in, in a corner, there sat a regular, alone, hidden behind a newspaper. An old gentleman with white sideburns and a red silk handkerchief sticking out of his breast pocket could be glimpsed in a mirror on the wall opposite. He was observing the waitress quietly and seriously. She was fat and red and white: red by nature, white with powder; resting her bosom and arms on the bar she looked like a sphinx.

The poet let out a sigh. Martin looked at him: a child's face and the red-bearded mask of a highwayman; he started to think he'd offended him just now and felt the need to say something friendly.

"You know what," he said, "if you shaved off that beard, I'm quite sure you'd look like an extraordinarily lecherous monk."

The poet lit up.

"You're probably right there," he said, and his eyes cast around for a mirror. "And I have, as a matter of fact, written poems that incline towards Catholicism. You ought to read my poems sometime, the real ones, the ones that can't be published."

"Yes," said Martin, "where do you live?"

The poet explained that he didn't live anywhere. He'd had no fixed abode for three weeks now and needed none. He wrote his poems in cafés and slept with girls, at one of whose places now was his green-striped overnight bag with a few spare collars and the poems of Verlaine, along with his own manuscripts.

Martin began to be genuinely impressed, but he found no expression for these feelings and silence once more descended on this pair, whom chance had brought together on a street corner.

The clock struck twelve, the gas lamps were turned half-way down, and, with the darkness, the poet felt inspiration take hold and started to write a verse at the table there and then.

Martin said goodnight.

Stureplan lay white and empty. It was no longer snowing; the moon was up, and it was even more bitterly cold than ever.

To the east a new street opened, a street with no buildings yet, like a huge hole in a wall. To the west, stretched out in the moonlit mist, was a snow-covered mass of old slums and gables, and from one of the cheap streets that crept forth between them a woman's laugh echoed, and the sound of a door that opened and was shut again.

## 10

It was late when Martin got home, and though dead tired he couldn't sleep. Black butterflies fluttered before his eyes, and thoughts and rhythms came to him as he lay there staring out into the dark. He rose in his bed and lit the candle on the bedside table, where pen and paper lay, as always, to hand. He felt no fever or frenzy, only a deep weariness that, though it might pain him, did not deceive; he saw clearly where his thoughts faltered and needed the support of a rhythm, a snatch of melody; he altered and rewrote, and at last he had a poem.

You up there,
deaf and dumb,
you up there,
squeezing your right hand
round the fragrant fresh fruit of goodness
and with your left pressing
the worm's nest of evil, heavy with a noisome stink,
and looking with equal satisfaction
on them both!
You up there,
whose eyes are dark
with all the empty blackness of space

— I've a prayer for you.

One prayer, just one,
that you cannot hear
and cannot answer:
Teach me,
teach me to forget
that I ever saw your face.
Because, you see,
in days gone by I
fashioned myself a god
in my own image,
a warm and living and fighting god
and I went walking one spring day,
searching heaven and earth for him.
It wasn't him I found,
it was you:
not the godhead of life
but death's god I found
under the mask of life.

Take it away,
the memory of that sight,
dread one! The memory
is a secret fever, a worm
eating away the root of the tree
of my life.
I know it well, with every year I squander
and every day that vainly passes:
it gnaws closer
to the nerve of my being.
It gnaws and consumes
everything in me of human nobility,
everything that dares, everything that

wills and acts
and it doesn't spare
the wondrous fragile compass of the soul
that points to good and evil.

Tell me, you up there,
is it your will
to refashion me in your image?
Was that what you meant
when you said:
He who has looked upon the face of God
must die?
Dread one,
won't you think again
before you contaminate
me, child of man,
with your sacred flaws?


II


The afternoon sun raked across the desk, gilding everything, the ink stand and the books and the words he wrote on the paper. Smoke from the chimneys rose straight and steady up into the sky, and in a window opposite a young Jewess was playing with her child.

Martin was writing to his sister.


*Dear Maria*

*Thank you for your letter. Mum's not well, as usual, but perhaps a little better these past few weeks. Dad is the same as ever, he just gets quieter with every passing year. So it's pretty tranquil here at home, for as you know I'm not much one for tittle-tattle myself either. Silence is golden! Unfortunately Uncle Janne and Auntie Louise etc are still alive and in good health, which by the way doesn't matter because we don't seem to be in line to inherit anything from them anyway. But they constantly torment me with questions about my prospects at work, whether dad can't expect a knighthood soon, whether your husband really does take morphine etc etc. There's no harm in them, of course, apart from that.*

*You asked if I was writing much nowadays — no, very little, but I've obtained a long-term appointment as a senior assistant, and last night I had a very vivid dream in which dad and I got a joint knighthood, because the king didn't have the means to give us one each.*

*Thanks for the invitation to stay over summer, but I doubt I'll be able to get away — most likely the appointment will last all summer. Sorry to hear your husband's having such trouble with his nerves. Glad your little lad's thriving.*

*Best from us all.*

*Your brother Martin.*


He put the letter in an envelope and set it aside.

He sat thinking about his sister. He asked himself: Is she happy? And inevitably he answered: No, she is not happy. Perhaps she doesn't realise it herself. Six years ago she was very happy, when she married, became the wife of a doctor and got her own little home in the country to run — just what she'd always dreamt of. And since then there'd been no sudden descent from that pinnacle of happiness: she'd just slowly drifted down, the way it usually happens as the years go by. Her husband is kind and talented and a skilful doctor, but he often clashes with the rich folk in his district and most of his patients are poor: so money's sometimes tight. Beyond that, I'm afraid his health has been undermined and his mood occasionally somewhat embittered. Still, he seemed to be in pretty good spirits when he was last up here in town on his own, without her. He had all the fun he could get, and I'm afraid he may have been a little unfaithful to her.

A rare bird, happiness . . .

As he was thinking these thoughts he once more began writing. He wrote slowly, only half serious, a sentence here and there, without really knowing where he wanted it to go.

*You don't know me. I saw you one day in the sunshine. That was weeks ago — months in fact. You were walking on the sunny side of the street; you were walking alone with your head bowed and smiling to yourself.*

*It was one of those days when the snow starts to melt on the streets and the pavements shine brilliant and wet. You stopped at a street corner to greet an old lady and you talked to her. The old lady was very ugly and very stupid, and I think she was a bit nasty too, as stupid people usually are. But when you looked at her and spoke to her, she at once became less ugly and less nasty.*

*A bit further up the street it was a gentleman who saluted you and you nodded your head in greeting. I felt my heart go bitter with jealousy, and my eyes followed him as he walked on along the street; but you couldn't see it in him, that he'd just exchanged a greeting with you: you'd simply have thought he was a lieutenant who'd just saluted a major.*

I've often seen you since that day. You don't know me, and it's not likely that you ever will come to know who I am. You walk in the sunshine; I, for the most part, walk in the shade. I dress the same as many other men do, and I'm always sure to observe you in such a way you won't notice me. No, you can't discover who I am.

You have a lamp with a yellow shade. Yesterday you were standing in the yellow light of that lamp for a long time, looking at the stars. You went to the window to roll down the blinds but for a little while you forgot yourself. Right in front of your window there was a star, shining brighter than the others. I couldn't see it from where I was, lodged in a little dark doorway opposite the building where you live, but I know where it is on spring evenings, this star, and that you must be able to see it from your window. It's Venus.

You don't know me, and I don't know you either, any more than I know any of those women who sometimes bring me great pleasure by visiting me at night in my dreams. That is why I'm addressing you so familiarly. But for a while now, out of all these women, you've been the only one, the others have abandoned me and I too, for my part, feel no longing for them.

Read this letter and think nothing of it; burn it if you will, or hide it at the bottom of your little secret drawer if you prefer. Read it and think nothing more about it, walk in the sunshine as you did before and smile in your own happy thoughts. But don't show it to your girlfriends and let them giggle and titter at it. If you do, then for three nights in a row you won't be able to sleep for evil dreams, and a little devil from hell will sit on the edge of your bed and watch you from dusk till dawn.

But I know you won't do that; you won't show it to anyone. Good night, my love. Good night!

Martin sat for a long time with the letter in his hand. *What might it lead to if I send it?* he asked himself. To nothing, presumably. It would set her imagination going a bit, her girlish yearnings might get a little nudge in the direction of the new and unknown. She perhaps would show the letter to her girlfriends, what with belief in devils being on the wane nowadays; but she wouldn't burn it. She might make fun of it, she might even consider it her duty to feel insulted; but in reality it would make her happy, and if, in the natural course of things, she marries and has children and the routine chores and worries of domestic life age her and with every year she sinks deeper into the comfortless monotony of existence, then she'll remember this letter and wonder who wrote it and perhaps whether it wasn't there that the true seed of happiness lay buried. And she won't even recall that it ever vexed her. And in truth it doesn't contain anything that reasonably could offend her. It simply shows her that a man desires her; and considering she's twenty years old and from head to toe an exceptionally beautiful and glorious one of nature's creations, she must already have noticed that men desire her. And that annoys her not at all, but rather makes her contented and happy, which is why she walks in the sunshine and smiles.

Thinking these things he nevertheless sat for a long time with the letter in his hand, weighing it as if it were a man's fate, until at last he found his hesitation ridiculous, put the letter in a thick, opaque envelope and wrote in a gracile, anonymous, girl's hand on the outside to avoid rousing any curiosity among her relations. He had, without disclosing any unusual interest, managed to discover her name. She was called Harriet Skotte. Her father had a property in the country, towards Lake Mälaren, and now, over winter, she was living with family in Stockholm to take a course in something — French, or dressmaking or some such: to get engaged, in other words.

Harriet Skotte. He repeated the name to himself and tried to discern the impressions it brought forth. He fixed on her Christian name especially and muttered, "Harriet, Harriet . . ." But it gave no real idea of her essence, it roused only a vague impression of something English and pale and blonde, of steam from a teacup, charity, cold bedrooms and varnished floors, as in a hospital. Her surname led merely to thoughts of her family, to an uncle at the Board of Trade, and a cousin who was a lieutenant in the Service Corps. But when he whispered her full name — Harriet Skotte — then a new element was introduced that entirely supplanted the others, something quite different and quite new: then he felt as if she herself were walking round the room with her brown hair shining in the shafts of sunlight . . .

He startled at the ringing doorbell; he could hear the maid going to answer, and a familiar voice asking if he was at home. He shoved the letter into his pocket and the next moment the door opened and Henrik Rissler stood on the threshold, blinded by the sun, whose copper-red rays now streamed in horizontally across the room.

12

Henrik Rissler had come down from Uppsala. He'd just completed his master's degree and now, in a few weeks, would set out on a tour of Europe before beginning his doctoral thesis, *On Romantic Irony*. He'd no fortune himself, but his uncle — managing director of a bank, politician and millionaire — had offered to pay for his travels. All this Martin knew already from Henrik's letters. But before leaving he was going to have a few weeks' rest. He was a little overstrained, having done so much work to get away from Uppsala as quickly as possible, but he'd still had time to write a few critical studies for a journal, thereby acquiring a modest reputation among the couple of dozen people who interested themselves in such things.

Martin had been expecting him for a few days and had a bottle of wine and a cigarette box ready.

Henrik shaded his eyes from the sun.

"Everything here's just the same as ever," he said. "Time's stood still!"

"Yes, more or less," Martin replied. "They've just built one big factory chimney right over there. It's been a great consolation to me in my solitude. There was a time I raced the builders in my writing, but I got left behind. I started a poem when they'd just started the chimney; now the chimney's finished, but not the poem. And it's beautiful — the chimney, I mean. Especially in the twilight, as a silhouette: the smoke no longer billows out, and you forget what it's there for; it's not a chimney, but a towering pillar, built by some Babylonian prince and priest, who climbs up there when night falls to measure the course of the stars.

"Indeed," said Henrik, "you forget the point of it and only then does it become beautiful!"

"No," said Martin, "it's not that it becomes beautiful because you forget its purpose, but because you aestheticise it into something else, something with a long and revered poetic tradition on its side. Anyway, factory chimneys are among the most beautiful of all modern buildings, aestheticising notwithstanding. Their substance exceeds their pretence, and indeed they disavow masks of any kind, Gothic or Renaissance . . ."

Henrik smiled.

"Very 'eighties'," he said.

Henrik Rissler sat in his old place in the corner of the couch, Martin sat in the rocking chair by the desk. They drank wine and talked about Uppsala, about books and women, and about a new philosopher by the name of Nietzsche. And as they spoke the shaft of sunlight, in which the dust danced like red sparks, grew ever more slender and oblique, and ever more fiercely red.

Martin observed Henrik. He found him changed. His face was leaner, more sharply defined, of a more masculine form. Why had he said, 'Everything here's just the same as ever. Time's stood still'? Clearly time had not stood still for *him*. He'd been through some experience, but what? He was in love, presumably; he might even be engaged — to whom? Was it his cousin Anna Rissler? She liked him, Martin knew that . . . No, most likely not . . . Was it Maria Randel or Sigrid Tesch?

"It's odd," said Henrik, "have you ever felt the same thing? How unpleasant it is to go in search of old moods and feelings and not find them? Rereading a book you liked, or hearing an opera which once you could put your heart and soul into, and a bit more besides, and sitting there empty-handed wondering, where did it all go?"

"Yes," said Martin, "it's a strange and distressing experience. You feel duty bound to stay true to your past, as if otherwise you'd be committing an act of disloyalty . . . And yet you can't help it. And why in fact is it so distressing? Is it perhaps that there's no injured party to bring suit for such an act, no determinate case to answer? Because the injured party is not the book or the music you've lost the taste for, nor the sphere of feeling that eludes you: the injured party is your own old self, and that, of course, is dead and gone. The new one has erased and overwritten it; it has no claim to pursue, and yet it does pursue some sort of claim — which is a contradiction, and there's nothing quite so distressing as a contradiction, unless it's merely ridiculous."

Henrik continued this line of thought: "Indeed you're right, the conflict is between present and former selves, and so long as there's a new self of greater strength you can always keep the shadows at bay. There's a constant state of flux: the old departs and the new arrives; well, the old departs: that, actually, is the only certain thing; how long can you be sure the new will come to take its place? Suppose one day the supply dries up, suppose nothing under the sun is new any more and you just grow poorer with every year and every day that passes!"

"Yes," said Martin, "sometimes such things happen. And when they do there's a danger you revert to the very oldest, the deadest and the most wizened, and you start to idolise it anew without noticing the caricature — that's probably the worst thing of all. Much better to heed the old adage: poor, but proud."

For a few moments they sat in silence. The sun was gone, but dusk had not yet fallen; in the room it almost seemed brighter than a while before: everything there had simply grown suddenly pale.

Henrik broke the silence.

"Yes," he said, "it's a wistful feeling to grow out of yourself and your old worlds of emotion — but what does it matter, so long as you keep on growing? And in any case, what is wistfulness if not what the rabble said about toothbrushes: a new form of indulgence the upper classes have dreamt up? Besides, it's only wistfulness when it's confined to emotions and music and ideas. And it's actually something else I've had in mind all along: I was thinking about women and love. Now, in that department it's not just wistfulness we're talking about — no, you don't get off so lightly. You're in love with a woman; you want to immerse yourself in that feeling for all eternity. But you can't escape the thought that that feeling too must be surrendered according to the same law of change that everything else in the world is subject to, and that one day you'll weary of the one you love, just as you've wearied of the moonlight music in *Faust*. I've not had many love affairs, but believe me, I have never, even in my imaginings, begun the game other than with the silent prayer: *May she be the first to weary, not I!*"

"I'm afraid, generally speaking, that prayer is not answered," said Martin. "No doubt both a lover and a married man can be deceived, but it surely rarely happens when they'd welcome it."

"And yet I'm ashamed of my prayer, because I know it comes straight from the great cowardice of my heart. How far must you have travelled from the plain and straightforward conception of these things when you find it pleasanter to be cheated on than to cheat? But so it is with me. What does love actually mean for me — what does it mean for men in general? How *could* there be anything tragic in being deceived in love? We all know that a man who takes it as a tragedy makes himself comical. If the discovery that he's a cuckold makes a man interrupt his reading of a good book then he deserves what he's got. Now, women . . . with them it's different."

Henrik's eyes stared out into emptiness.

"Betrayed women, deserted women," he said, "there's something about them. It's not easy to move on from them — Oh, well, if they bicker and wrangle and make a scene, then of course it's easier at once, then the whole thing's a pantomime and you just shake it off and you're free. When that happens you're left asking yourself: how could I ever have loved that person? And then it's easy to convince yourself that you never did love her and then she's right out of the picture. But the others . . . the most distressing thing of all, it seems to me, is to imagine the girl I love wizened and pale, despised, living on the seamy side of life, while I myself move on to higher things . . . It's a paradox, I know, something that cannot happen; you can't at one and the same time *act* thus and *feel it* thus. And yet . . . I just encountered an old woman, here on the street, just outside the front door of this very building. She was old and deathly pale and faintly absurd. She was dressed very shabbily, well born, but now poor. You see old women like that often enough, there was nothing special about her, nothing that would distinguish her from the many others of her kind — except that suddenly, as I approached her, it struck me that she so resembled . . . Well now, I might just as well come right out with it. There's a certain young lady I'm very fond of. I'm so fond of her that we're going to get married, perhaps very soon. And it was her the old woman resembled, the great difference in age and everything else notwithstanding. It was, incidentally, one of those vague resemblances you see one moment and find gone the next — without then being able to say just what it was. But that single moment was enough for me, a shiver ran through me, an icy shiver, as if I'd never seen anything so dreadful — and because everything else was so normal, the sun shining, people walking on the street, it seemed all the worse . . . The girl I like stood before me and passed by me, wizened and despised and faintly absurd. Even the thought that I myself would be dead and lying six feet under was no consolation; only the thought that I would be living on, just as pitiable and decrepit as her, brought any comfort."

For a long time they sat in silence.

"Tell me," said Martin at last, "who is she, this girl you're fond of? If you can tell me. Do I know her?"

"Yes," replied Henrik quietly, "you do know her, and you I can tell. She's Sigrid Tesch."

Sigrid Tesch. Martin pictured a young, slight figure with rich dark hair and a distinguished, well-proportioned face. He'd met her a few times, always in passing. He knew she'd made an impression on Henrik, and she'd occasionally featured in twilight thoughts of his own with a pale, dreamy smile.

So, Sigrid Tesch was the one who'd be Henrik's bride.

"Yes," said Henrik, "isn't it inexplicable, you don't dare get mixed up in something like love, and yet . . . ?"

"Indeed," said Martin, "and yet . . ."

They both smiled.

Henrik Rissler rose.

"It's gone dark," he said, "we can barely see the glasses. Do you want to go for a walk with me? It'll be lovely out this evening. Ah, yes, you have to write — see you soon, then. Farewell!"

## 13

It was gloomy now, almost dark, and still Martin sat in the rocking chair at the desk, unable to bring himself to light the lamp. There was still a little wine in the bottle; he poured it into his glass and drank. He'd opened the window to let the smoke drift out, and amid the sound of tramping feet rising from below like a hundred ticking clocks, he heard the street door open and close again and footsteps departing into the distance — Henrik's. Martin thought about Henrik's love and what he'd said of it, and suddenly it struck him that his own infatuation, at the slightest contact with this grain of reality, had dissolved and vanished like mists and dreams. Harriet Skotte . . . He asked himself: If tomorrow I were to read in the newspaper that she's engaged, or married, or that she's dead — what would that mean to me? Nothing, no reality hollowed out — not even a shattered hope, just a bubble that burst and would have burst anyway soon enough.

He took the letter he'd written out of his pocket, opened it and read it again. *I'll burn it,* he thought. *Well, why burn it? I might be able to find a use for it sometime, in a short story.*

He cast it in a desk drawer among other manuscripts. And once more he sank back into his dreams.

Suddenly his mother was standing in the doorway. She was holding a lamp, and she leaned forward and looked at him.

"You're sitting in the dark," she said. "Dad's gone out. Might I sit with you here awhile?"

Martin nodded. She put the lamp on the desk, got her sewing basket and her needles and began to sew.

For a long time she sat there in silence, bowed over her work. At last she raised her head, and her eyes were wide with tears and sleepless nights.

"Martin," she said, "you mustn't be cross, but one day, when you were out, I couldn't help but open up one of your desk drawers and look at your papers. I'd never know what you were thinking about otherwise. And what I found so upset me I had to sit down and cry. I didn't understand it, I didn't even know if they were meant to be poems or what they were meant to be, I just thought they were full of terrible blasphemies. I was so scared, for a while I almost thought you'd lost your mind. Oh I know I don't understand anything, but even I can tell you'll never get anywhere writing things like that. And you can write so beautifully when you want to!"

Martin was silent. What could he say? He felt, or at any rate thought, that mother had actually wanted to say something quite different, that this 'never getting anywhere' was merely an expedient she seized when thoughts and words failed her. She had no doubt felt and sensed that the writings she found were meant to be understood quite otherwise than she was now affecting to believe; she wanted him to explain himself, to talk to her about his thoughts — she was banging on the door: *Let me in, don't let me stand outside, freezing, I'm so lonely!* But he didn't open the door; he couldn't — he'd never closed it, it had simply locked itself. What answer could he give her? Her words filled him with deep despond. If he had one ambition it was to write so that anyone with a little good-will could understand. He'd no taste for literary elitism, he couldn't believe in a literature for the select, nor had it escaped his notice how readily it turned out that nobody wanted to be among that select . . . Now, at once, he saw clearly how hopeless his ideal was, that there was no such thing as art for all or ideas for all — on the contrary, the simplest ideas in the plainest language were only rarely understood by anyone other than those already familiar with the relevant sphere of thought. How could he talk to her about his ideas when her vocabulary, shaped as it was by the monotony of the years, didn't even suffice to express what she herself thought and felt deep within? The god he'd written about was the god of Spinoza, the World Soul — but of course that god was just a thought experiment, whereas hers, his mother's, was a creation of imaginative fantasy, and as such had always had a little more life and a little more blood. How could he explain to her that the things she called blasphemies weren't directed at her god at all? She would have answered that there was only one god. Martin knew everything she would say in reply, and so he remained silent, looking out through the window and listening to the tired tramping of feet on a Saturday evening down there on the street and to the rain that had started to fall on the window sill. And to what she had said about his future, what response could he make? Of course there was only one response: to be a success, to become famous. And that response he could not make. *If one day I do achieve something,* he thought, *some success that could make her happy, it'll most likely come when she's no longer around to enjoy it. That's the way it always goes. Why should I hope for an exception for her and me?* So what, then, should he do? Should he put his arms round her neck and stroke her hair and kiss her? No, that wouldn't seem right. He didn't like that sort of theatrics and neither did she; he knew her, she'd never be satisfied with it. She had asked, and what she expected was an answer. He could make no answer, and he remained silent.

He remained silent, and at the same time he felt the silence aching in his heart, and because he could say nothing instead his eyes sought out hers, which once had smiled so bright and blue when they looked at his. Indeed it still happened sometimes, in the middle of dinner or over tea in the evenings, that she looked at him and nodded and smiled, bright as ever, just as mothers nod and smile at their tiny children before they can talk. Perhaps she had a sense that time had run in a circle and that this smiling was the only means of expression left to her when she wanted to communicate with her child. And it was in just that way that he wished she would want to look at him now, and nod her head, and smile: with a smile far on the other side of all the insignificant things that divided them.

But she did not smile. She sat quietly, with her hands folded in her lap, and her eyes, which otherwise had been so close to tears, stared tearlessly into the shadows as if seeking and asking: *Are all mothers as unhappy as I? As lonely? As much abandoned by their children?*

The lamp's flame flickered abruptly in the night wind. She rose and said goodnight, took the lamp and left.

14

Still Martin sat by the window.

Time has stood still here: that's what Henrik Rissler said. Indeed, he was right. Here time stood still. We measure the passing of time by changes, and I have nothing to measure it with. I wouldn't even know it was Saturday today if it weren't for hearing those footsteps down there.

He began thinking of an old story. Once upon a time there was a sinner, and one evening he died in his bed. The next morning he woke up in hell, rubbed his eyes and cried: 'What time is it?' And then the Devil was standing by his side and smiling and he held up a clock for him, a clock with no hands. Time was over, eternity had begun.

Eternity; no more need to rush . . .

Other people have day and night, weekend and workday, Christmas and Easter. For me it all runs together as one. Am I living in eternity already?

And he thought on: Tomorrow it's Sunday. What does that mean for me? It means that tomorrow I'm free from my ostensible work, and that I therefore feel the claims of what ought to be my real work twice as strongly. But if the weather is nice, I shall of course go out for a walk . . . So it won't be a proper Sunday whatever I do. What a strange sort of work it is I've taken on! Wouldn't it be best to renounce it while there's still time, to submit to the rule that governs everyone else? I'll never be done with it, never enjoy a sense of rest and ease. No end of days free, but never a true Sunday, never again!

My ostensible work and my real work — how long will I be able to maintain this pretence? The truth is that I'm well on the way to securing a permanent appointment, that in eight or ten years' time I'll have it, and in forty I can retire on a pension. My poor mother would be spared many qualms if she saw all this as clearly as I do now. But in the innocence of her heart she really does believe that if I scribble a few notes of an evening it'll get in the way of my advancement, because she has no conception of humanity's boundless indifference to ideas. To harm my prospects I'd have to write some personal abuse aimed at my superiors, and why would I do that? They're mild-mannered people who've directed remuneration and bonuses my way, notwithstanding that others have deserved them better. They've no doubt taken a liking to me. I'll never be one to upset the apple cart, and they sense as much instinctively and are presumably right.

He felt he would vanish into the pack. He could not decide whether, fundamentally, he was just like everyone else and that this fate was therefore the lot he deserved, or whether perhaps he was so much of an exception that he couldn't make a mark even among exceptions; he simply felt that the *rule* bound him more tightly with every day that passed, and that he would vanish into the pack. And this other thing, his writing — what was it, and where might it lead? Once, when he needed money, he'd gathered up a bundle of his poems and taken them round to publishers. A couple had wanted them, but none wanted to pay anything. "No," he had responded with great earnestness, "I'm not that desperate to see my name in print!" When he got home he glanced through these poems again, and again, as so often before, found them vacuous and bland. Most had been written with a view to immediate sale to a newspaper and it showed. And he said to himself: How equivocal it is to be busying oneself with ideas when one's own livelihood isn't assured! As deftly as the priest in his funeral oration recasts the deceased's meal ticket as his mission in life, no less swiftly and mercilessly does the world transform the life's work of a man with no independent means into his meal ticket. And if then it does at least become a genuine meal ticket . . . but no, it doesn't, it turns to disgust and loathing and you tire of it altogether and you sink back, down into the pack.

Down into the pack . . . doing as others do: at least then you can dispense with illusions, you can recover your sense of time, weekends and weekdays, work and rest, real rest . . .

The night air streamed in cold through the window, and Martin froze but he couldn't bring himself to reach out and close it. Still the rain was spitting and as so often, when he was very tired, his thoughts started to proceed in metre and rhyme.

> I'm sitting alone in the dark
> And hearing the falling rain
> The sound of the water that drips
> Against my window pane.
>
> My chest is oppressed with a dread
> An anguish that never stops
> For these are the days of my youth
> Running away in drops.

# III

## The Winter Night

I

Above Martin's table in his office an electric light with a green
shade was swinging slowly back and forth on its silken cord
like a pendulum. It had been set in motion when he switched it
on, a few seconds before. He didn't reach out his hand to
steady it, but calmly awaited the moment when the oscillation
would fade into imperceptibility. Lights were being turned on
above other tables too: six glowing green triangles swayed
slowly back and forth in the dusk of the room, and by the
windows the lean hands of scribes fumbled for the cords that
would draw the blinds and shut out the snow and the winter
gloom. Martin loved these green lamps that didn't get hot or
smell vile and whose light had the pure cold sheen of a gem-
stone's, and he longed for the day when electric light would
become cheap enough to find its way into the homes of the
poor. And precisely here, in this large, low-ceilinged old room
with its whitewashed walls, precisely because the building was
old and had a cross vault in its portico and squat, small-paned
windows in its entresol — where his office stood — it seemed
to him that these green lamps sat still more agreeably with the
tenor of their surroundings; he saw in this a symbol of the
continuity of progress, an unbroken chain of hands and aspirations, from those who'd long since wearied to those who were
still unborn, the new embedded in the fabric of the old . . . For
where everything is old an atmosphere of despond and decay
prevails, and where everything is new, only those who are new
from tip to toe, from wallet to soul, can feel at home and thrive.

And Martin was not new; his clothes were not new and
nor were his thoughts: he thought and understood not much

more than others had taught him, a few old gentlemen in England and France who now were mostly dead. And if these thoughts still gave him some pleasure, it was because the times seemed long since to have forgotten them, as if they'd been written in running water. Now different winds prevailed, winds that had him turning up his collar over his ears, everything rose again, and all the revenants looked on, but Martin didn't want to see them.

The lamp above his table had stopped swaying, and he returned to his sums. He was no longer satisfied with just making ticks; he conscientiously checked every entry and added up every column. He'd long overcome the disdain for mechanical tasks of his earliest youth, and he'd gradually found that these calculations were absolutely not, as he'd first thought, free from the imperfection that attaches to all that is human. On the contrary, they were often marred by irregularities and errors; and when, once in a while, he discovered such an error, his heart gladdened, but at the same time he felt a distant pang of sorrow. He gladdened at the opportunity to demonstrate his great zeal, and because he could count on his entitlement to a certain percentage of the sum which his attentiveness had recovered for the coffers of the state; and he sensed a dim memory of old sorrow when he recalled that once, long ago, he'd desired quite different sorts of pleasures from life. Occasionally too he considered the poor functionary off in Landskrona or Åhus or Haparanda who had miscalculated, perhaps under the influence of yesterday's grog, and who now would have to pay. But this thought did not move him, for the years had taught him the need to set limits on one's sympathy.

It was warm in the room. In the stove the remnants of a big blaze of birchwood were still glowing: there was no reason to spare the Crown's firewood when the season demanded economising on fuel at home; and the head clerk, von Heringslake, who earned 4,600 kronas in interest each year and discharged his office with the agreeable insouciance of a man of independent means, was squatting down in front of the stove and roasting apples on the embers. In the shiny crown of his head — which his deadly enemy Registrar Camin claimed to be the fruit of earlier debauchery, but which in reality glowed with the innocence of earliest childhood — there gleamed the triangular reflection of a green lamp. The aroma of roasted apples filled the air and saturated Martin's sense of smell, and it grieved him bitterly that he had not in all things the same opinions on this life and the next as Heringslake, because if he had he would certainly have been offered an apple. From Registrar Camin's place came for the hundredth time the vatic old pronouncement that the country will never prosper until we impose taxes on farmers. And at the lowest table, off by the door, where it was draughty and smelled musty from the umbrellas and overcoats, the youngest generation was eagerly at work putting ticks in the margins while at the same time whisperingly trying to recall last night's revelry and the number of drinks consumed.

Martin was still young, for in the service of the state one ages slowly; but he was no longer one of the youngest and was no longer required to sit in the draught by the door. He was on first-name terms with most of his immediate superiors and older colleagues, and he likewise did not shirk his duty to establish such informal relations with those who were younger than he. This would normally happen at a special shared evening meal in December — now just days away, and the guest list was currently circulating in the office; but Martin did not sign up. He had another use for his money, and among the newcomers there was only one with whom he particularly wanted to be on closer terms, a young man who sat opposite him at his table and about whom there was something that seemed to have a certain familiarity and roused his instinctive sympathy: the empty, dreamy gaze, the mechanical gesture with which ticks were marked. Martin would often speak to him about the goings on in the world and was pleased when, occasionally, he received an intelligent response. Now he handed him the guest list without adding his own name to it, and the younger colleague looked up and asked, in a tone perhaps expressing slight disappointment, "You're not coming to the party?"

"No," said Martin. "I'm otherwise engaged. But you and I need not stand on ceremony, we can address one another by our Christian names anyway."

The other man blushed a little, and then the two shook hands across the table.

"Tell me," said the younger man after a little while, "why does Registrar Camin want to tax the farmers?"

"To be honest I don't think he does," replied Martin. "I expect he knows well enough that taxing farmers will raise the price of food even more than customs duty does. He's simply repeating an old adage he heard in his youth when he was an assistant. He took a shine to it because it gives expression to a collective antipathy, a class hatred; and the mediocre man always needs to love and hate by the group. Pay heed to that: it's one of the surest signs of a shallow mind. He likes women, civil servants, the highest-ranking actors at the Royal Theatre, and people from Västergötland — being one himself; he hates farmers, Jews, Norwegians and newspaper journalists. It's true that the farmers compensate the services he and the rest of us here at the office render our country a little stingily, and that's the main reason he hates them. But in that they follow the same principle as all other employers: pay as little as the market will bear. Should civil servants ever be in short supply, they'd pay more. "

Von Heringslake, who'd now eaten his roast apples and retaken his seat at the table nearest Martin, turned round on his chair and regarded him dolefully.

"You've no heart," he said.

It was past three o'clock; here and there people were gathering their papers and leaving. Martin rose, took his coat and his hat, turned off his green lamp and went. There was a mourning ribbon on his hat, because his mother was dead.

2

He went via Västerlånggatan. On snowy days he almost always took this route; in the narrow winding passages between the tall old buildings you were halfway towards being indoors, in the lee of the worst gusts.

*Winter, the cold* . . . it's odd there are people who maintain they like this kind of weather. Heringslake, a big-hearted man who loves his country, thinks the cold preferable to warmth. But when it is cold he always wraps himself up in furs. The notion of hell as a very warm place clearly betrays its origins in the hot parts of the world; if the northerners had invented hell it would instead be some wretched draught hole, a reservoir of influenza and chronic catarrh. But that's just the way our climate is, I've accustomed myself to it, and perhaps it's rendered me valuable services that I don't even know about. You can, after all, put food on ice to preserve it, everything lasts longer in the cold, so why not people too? Once, I longed to be consumed by the flames of a great passion; it never appeared, maybe because I wasn't worthy of such a great honour, or whatever the reason . . . But now, later on, I've begun to suspect that such a conflagration is more a pyrotechnic display for the onlookers than any great pleasure for those involved. At any rate, it's clear that fire is not my element. If ever a true spring sun came into my life I'd probably go rotten at once, unaccustomed to the climate.

He stopped for a moment outside a jeweller's window. Most of the pieces were marked by vulgar taste, which made up for the fact that he couldn't afford them. Still, once, on this very day a year before, he'd bought a little ring with a green emerald. And she, the woman who received it, wore it still, and had no wish to wear another. She'd said she didn't even want a plain gold ring round her finger. Well, he wasn't in a position to offer her one in any case . . .

I'm ungrateful, he said to himself, a little sunshine has, after all, finally come into my life, perhaps more than appears in most. But I froze for such a long time, I've probably still not managed to thaw out yet.

He'd come out onto Mynttorget, and the northerly storm swept snow into his eyes again, and he groped his way towards Norrbro almost blind. Once more he had to stop to get his breath, by Looström's bookshop, where the celebrities of the day were set out in rows in the window: Francesco Crispi, King Milan of Serbia, and Hippolyte Taine, and between an Excellency and a forger he spotted a face that seemed familiar. It was a Swedish poet, the decadent who'd once elaborated his worldview to him over a green chartreuse at the *Anglais*. He earned his place there not because he'd become a famous man, but because he was dead.

Martin carried on homewards.

At last — someone who achieved his goal. His goal was a little unusual, and nor did he achieve it quite as he'd envisaged: he never attained the *paralysie générale* he dreamt of, but died of plain and simple TB. But I doubt he set much store by the details; in truth he just wanted to perish, regardless of the manner. And perhaps he was right: that's the kind of goal one ought to resolve upon to have a hope of achieving it in one's lifetime. True, you can also resolve to be a millionaire or a bishop or a cabinet minister, and those goals too are attainable, if you set your mind to it. The ones who understand, with sufficient force, the need to concentrate one's will on a single goal are so vanishingly few that the competition can hardly be intense. Everybody wants to be rich; but most people also want to live as if they already are — they want to take it easy, sleep in in the mornings, drink champagne with the girls and so on, and so they never do become rich — and they don't even become bishops or cabinet ministers either. The man who wants to stop here and there *en route* to enjoy life a bit before he reaches his goal never will reach it — and the others, the untiring travellers, the men of will, who reach theirs — what do they have left at journey's end? On the other hand, perhaps it's not necessary to expend any great energy on that poet's goal: to perish. That's a goal which quite certainly can be achieved at a lower price — it approaches anyway, slowly but surely. Best of all is perhaps what another dead man back there in that window loved so dearly while he was alive: a big tree and calm thoughts. For it's not quite true, what Guido Cavalcanti said as he felt death approaching, that thought and action are equally vain. It's no doubt true in a way — that is, the end result is always the same black cavern — and as a meditation on death Cavalcanti's words have a certain merit. But looked at another way, it's obvious that the man who relishes thinking, in this world of imponderables, is always a little better placed than the man of action: for the thinker every moment has a worth of its own, independent of any precarious future goal. A man who wants to be a Knight of the Seraphim or the Pope, and sacrifices everything, the pleasures of reflection and the pleasures of love, in pursuit of his goal — and the first sacrifice at least is unavoidable — and then gets a fishbone stuck in his throat and dies before reaching it — his life is nothing, an overture without an opera. But the man whose life centres on thought, his life can be cut off whenever you please and yet remain like the garden worm in folk belief: it thrives just as well, is just as viable, even cut up in pieces, as a fragment — indeed it probably never pretended to want to be anything but a fragment. For the man whose life centres on thought can never settle on any human goal, or, if occasionally he does, it's an insignificant and indifferent one and of no account whether he reaches it or not.

Martin had come up towards Östermalm and was almost home; he was hungry and longing for his dinner, but he nevertheless stopped at a street corner and looked up at a window high on the third floor.

Yes, the light was on; she was home: which, in any case, he knew already, as he knew that she would be expecting him after dinner. And in the evening they'd go to the theatre together and sit in a private box partly hidden behind trellis-work where nobody could see them.

Martin had got a girlfriend. Chance had brought them together. She worked at a life-insurance firm in the mornings, counting money. She worked for her own upkeep — she had indeed an elderly father somewhere off in the country, a retired forester who wrote to her three times a year, but she supported herself and was dependent on no one. Like other girls she'd long dreamt of a conventional happiness and she'd guarded her virtue and had hoped to marry. She'd had crushes and fallen in love with men who'd not even noticed; but these little flames had died out when no one stoked them, and had just one not entirely ridiculous or repellent man been minded to reach out his hand to her, she would probably have had no trouble convincing herself that she loved him. But she'd seen the years run by, and in winter she'd danced and in summer gone on cycle rides, and many men had given her cause to think, with hints and glances, that they wanted her; but none wanted to marry her, for she possessed no fortune and her family was not an influential one. Other men, the frugal and the socially unambitious, were nevertheless frightened off by her elegance, for she had fine and sure tastes and two dextrous hands, and many nights she would sit up by her lamp sewing cheap offcuts and scraps into dresses which to unpractised eyes appeared costly and which among one or two of the most sceptical even raised doubts about her virtue. But she was not sufficiently beautiful for men whose feelings are determined by their vanity, nor had her character any of the sheep-like complaisance that unerringly captures those who want to be masters of their house or have simply wearied of bachelor life and therefore look around for a nice and sweet and cheap and obedient wife. Her essential character and her external circumstances were thus both such that she had no great prospects of being loved for any reason other than love, and it had slowly started to dawn on her that this feeling, of which so much is spoken and written, was in reality repudiated and despised and extraordinarily rare. She had reflected on all this, had felt the minutes running through her fingers like sand, had realised that the years awaiting her would be yet more miserable and more worthless than those that had gone, and that the jewel she was guarding was losing its value with every day that passed. Most of all it frightened her how quickly women living without a husband age — unless they be the fortunate ones who feel no strong want or desire. But she was not among them; she was a real woman and she knew it. That desire, which in her earliest youth had been but a sweet and ill-defined longing, a dream of contentment of a rare and unknown kind, now burned like a poison in her blood; and those first shy girlish imaginings that scarcely dreamt beyond a twilight kiss among the rosebushes had with the years grown to a picture book much worse than the one the Sandman, in the fairytale, shows to the naughty children. Her gaze grew searching and inquiring, and she tried to steel herself to a resolve. She'd almost given up hope of a husband — she sought a lover, and even that quest was long in vain. There was no shortage of men to take her out dancing, indeed there were plenty, and she could have her pick. Her eyes ran round the circle, she flirted left and right. She grew less concerned about her reputation and she went to secret assignations with men who'd paid her attention some evening at a ball. But they remained strangers to her, and every time she approached a decision shame overpowered her and fear and repugnance abruptly made her cold as ice. For every time the moment came, she read in the man's eyes his heart's inexorable callousness: she read so clearly that it might have been written on white paper, that what for her would be a wholly new life, perhaps ruin, perhaps salvation, was for him an idle dalliance; she read that what she was about to commit was in his eyes actually an error, one he was prepared to overlook only so long as it gave him satisfaction; and she read that he not only intended to abandon her very soon, but meant also first to ease his conscience by showing her his contempt. She saw all this and tired of the game before it had yet begun, and she asked herself whether she ought not after all follow the path of virtue, which was in any case clearly the most untroubled, and grow old and wither without desire and without hope. But when she met Martin, everything changed, and when she gave herself to him she no longer felt fear, for she saw that he had understood her and his thoughts were not like the others', and she knew that he loved her. And before him she felt no shame, nor did she affect any, for she had already sinned so much in her thoughts that to her the reality seemed innocent and pure. She was no longer young — she, like Martin, was approaching thirty; her skin was already marked by the first frosts, and illusions undeceived had made her heart bitter and her tongue coarse. But that bitter heart beat warm and strong when it rested against his, and the coarse words made her lips no less sweet to kiss.

Martin sat alone with his father at the dining table, within the same circle of yellow light that had enveloped the sleepy winter evenings of his childhood. Martin Birck and his father rarely had anything to say to one another. They thought differently about everything, except customs duty on food. This lack of agreement brought them no sorrow, however: they attached almost no significance to it. They both knew that different generations think differently, and they found it natural. Nor did either of them find silence awkward or oppressive, it was merely the self-evident expression of the fact that nothing had happened to give rise to an exchange of views. When they did speak to one another it was mainly about promotions within the civil service and about new buildings: for Martin's father was interested in his city. On Sundays he'd often go for long walks to distant parts of the city and see new districts sprouting up out of the earth and think about how Stockholm had changed since his youth; and he thought all the new buildings very fine, especially if they were large and imposing and had lots of windows and little towers on the corners. And when Martin heard his father talk about all these ugly buildings and call them beautiful, he would think how unfair life was, barring the way to the innermost reaches of the land of beauty so implacably precisely to those who were the best and most useful members of society: for that path ran through melancholy — there was no other — and that Greek musician was not joking when he replied to Alexander: 'May the gods never make you so unhappy, sir, that you understand music better than I.' But Martin's father's youth had been weighed down with cares, and the years of his manhood laborious and burdened with duties, and so he never had come to know the melancholy with which life punishes those who think more about beauty and ugliness, and good and evil, than about their daily bread.

On this particular day his father also chatted about one thing and another over coffee and cigars. He spoke of a gentlemen's lunch he'd been to the day before, where he'd been embarrassed by the insignia of the Order of Vasa he'd been wearing — the large, official size, the only one he possessed — while all the other gentlemen had been wearing neat little versions.

"And so of course," he said, "I looked like the biggest fool there."

"Indeed," said Martin, "appearances were against you. But in reality the others' miniatures constitute precisely the sure proof that their folly is greater, because to acquire them they'd subjected themselves to expenses beyond what was strictly necessary."

"Yes," father responded, "that's what I thought too, but I felt ashamed anyway."

The conversation petered out. Martin had started to think of other stories he'd heard about orders of nobility: of the man who got the Order of Vasa because he'd sent flowers to Sofiahemmet on the days the queen was to be there, and the man who got the Polar Star for buying a house. But he couldn't bring himself to tell these stories because, on reflection, it seemed possible that what he found so amusing might not have quite the same effect on his father, who'd acquired his Order through forty years' meagrely rewarded work in the service of the state, and who therefore could hardly avoid regarding them with a certain seriousness, though he might outwardly share the joke.

The silence spread around them; father smoked his cigar and looked out into the darkness lurking beyond the windowpane, and Martin sat in thought. He was thinking about the history of his home, how, like others, it had come into being, grown and blossomed, and how then the flower had fallen, petal by petal: sister married, mother dead. The best time, the blossoming, is in most cases probably when the children have just grown up and the older ones are still not too old. True, he'd often heard old women saying that the happiest time is when the children are small; and perhaps for mothers that is true. But he recalled the years between his sister's growing up and her marriage. It was a happy home in those days: youth, friends, music. The piano, which now lay silent, still retained the waltzes and operatic medleys from years gone by, and often, when he lay awake at night, he could still hear in his mind the Norwegian songs they sang then, *Secret love* and *I don't ask for the rose by your breast*: songs in which a part of his youth still lived, and which now seemed filled with the strange melancholy of things past.

Then, all at once, it grew quieter, and then quieter still with every year, until one day father and son sat alone in an empty, fragmented home. And he looked at his father and asked himself: what can I be to him? Boundlessly little was the only possible answer. Virtually nothing. She, whom he'd loved from his earliest youth, now lay under the earth, beneath a little grey stone, covered with snow, and could not bring warmth to his old age. The fire in the hearth was on the way to dying out. He, Martin, was the one who ought to light a new flame. He felt it was just this, when in other respects life is running its normal course, that the old have the right to expect from the young: the right to see the next link in the chain forged, a new home, a grandchild to bounce on the knees. Such was the way nature had ordained things: above all it strives to conceal death behind new, young life, as we ourselves hide the corpse beneath flowers; oblivion is then easier to approach: the track veers downwards, indeed, but one walks it amid games and childish babbling, as one began. But to this great and simple demand Martin could make no reply. True, he knew this thing and that, indeed he didn't believe there existed any species of beauty in the world that was foreign to him, nor that there was any idea or any nuance of any idea that lay beyond his capacity to understand, and on top of all this he could scrutinise the national accounts and draw cartoons in the margins and drink a great deal of whisky without passing out, and perhaps some other little things besides. But he could not create a home of his own. There were no prospects, no plans in that direction. A craftsman or a factory worker could do it, but not he. He could not conjure forth the four thousand a year that a poor middle-class family needed to live. And if indeed he would be able to do it eventually, and with time he probably would, by then he'd already be old, and his father dead — and she, the woman he loved, what would have become of her?

But it was true, as he knew perfectly well, that at least consciously his father made no such claims on him. On the contrary, his father understood clearly how impossible it was. He held out no hope of seeing the continuation of his line, of growing old surrounded by the future and by promise and new shoots. But Martin knew that precisely this thing that was not to be hoped for lay over him as a dark sorrow and made his twilight years greyer and emptier still. He had no shortage of other cares. His daughter's marriage had brought but little joy: her boy was dead, and recently she'd written home saying she wanted to divorce her husband.

*The fire is dying out in the hearth, who will light the new flame?*

Father went to his room for a postprandial nap.

It was five o'clock, and Martin dressed to go to her who awaited him. He wore his best clothes, never mind that they'd be alone and seen by no one else. He'd promised her, because today was their anniversary.

# 4

She was standing by the dresser, where two slender candles were burning in front of the mirror; she'd just arranged her rich brown hair, and before she finished dressing ran the powder puff over her face to tame the reddest flushing. He was sitting behind her, on the couch, but their eyes met in the mirror and locked onto one another with a long smile. The shuddering of the candle flames, and the distance between them, lengthened in the mirror, made this smile dark and mysterious. And deep within the dark depths behind the mirror glass danced a green spark from the emerald on her finger.

"Are you going to be ready soon?" he asked. "It's getting on for half-past seven. I'm afraid we'll be late for the ghost."

They were off to see *Hamlet*.

She turned and stroked his face with the powder puff, so he turned white as a Pierrot.

"Silly Pierrette," he said, and he wiped the powder off with her handkerchief, "can't you see I'm pale enough already?"

She bent over, pressed his head against her breast and kissed his hair.

"I'm so happy," she whispered, "because today is my anniversary, and because I'm going to go to the theatre with you and sit in a little corner where no one will see us."

He gently caressed her hand. He felt a secret pang in his heart when he heard her talking so, because he sensed and he knew that had it been at all possible she'd much rather have sat with him where everyone could see them. But he didn't believe she'd been thinking of such things just now. Not once in the past year had she dropped even a hint about marriage, and of course she knew all too well how impossible it was. But Martin could never cease to feel it as a secret shame that it was beyond his power to bestow on her the happiness that lay in a respected and secure status, and in not having to hide anything from the world. And he felt this, not because there lurked in a corner of his soul some notion of a duty to fulfil or of an offence to make amends for, but because he loved her immensely and so wanted to make life bright for her eyes and smooth for her little feet, which had had such stony paths to tread that it was no surprise if she'd finally worn down her shoes.

But he pushed such thoughts aside; in any case he had no intention of taking on the impossible, he was not a strong man, not a man to take her in his arms and forge a path for them both. And of course it was she who had chosen him. She'd known strong men too, the sort of man about whom women say: he's a *real* man; and if she'd wanted she could have given her love to one of them, and they would not have rejected it. But her innermost instincts had pushed her back with premonitions of misery and shame. For, oddly enough, it is just those strong men who would be least likely to act as Martin would have acted had he been able: they are strong precisely because in the end, when the chips are down, their feelings always align with their own advantage; and for the most part they know where that advantage lies. No, there was nothing other for them to do, this cold and lonely pair, than warm themselves on the happiness that had fallen into their hands, gratefully and without making any demands on the impossible, and bless the day when for the first time they were driven together by the voice of the blood that told them they fitted one another and could bring one another joy. But still Martin secretly tarried, gladly and often, with the remote dream that one day, many years hence, he might be able to give her a home. The thought that by that time she would already be an old woman did not frighten him. He had a feeling that, however time rushed by, though she might get lines by her eyes and grey in her hair, her young white body could never grow old, that it would forever remain slender and young and warm as now, and that however the years might pass and winter upon winter bury his youth in snow and prick his soul and his thoughts with icicles, his heart would always be warmed by the beat of hers, as now, and that whenever they came together they would always strike a spark of the sacred fire that warms up all the world.

And as he was thinking all this his eyes were following every move of her slender white arms before the mirror, and again his smile sought hers, and she nodded at him with a glimmer of secret happiness colouring her skin still, beneath the powder, and deep into the darkness he could see his own face, features etched to a mask-like angularity by the candle-light, nodding in reply like a Chinese doll.

"There's no hurry," she said. "In any case, we hardly dare slip into our little box until they're a good way through the first act, otherwise we might run into people we know in the corridors."

"Yes, you're right," he replied. For that matter, he too had had the same thought.

"You've got to have your wits about you when you're in our position," she nodded, "it's not as if we're just sitting inside reading. But when you think about it, isn't it almost miraculous: we've been left in peace for a whole year, and nobody knows a thing! I even think there's less gossip about me now than before. Everyone's been so friendly to me, the chief cashier and the treasurer and the girls in the office. But perhaps it's because I'm prettier than before — I am aren't I? I'm sure they can tell I'm happy, and it softens them up and makes them nice and kind to me without their having the faintest idea why. Imagine if they found out!"

Martin wasn't fond of hearing her talking about her happiness. It was one thing to read it in her eyes and her skin and feel it in her kisses — then he believed in it, and no scripts could be sweeter to decipher than those. But when he heard her say it out loud he felt a weight of bitterness and oppression over his chest at the thought of how little he actually had to give her and how full of rents and flaws her poor happiness was, and he knew that these short minutes she spent with him brought such colour to her cheeks precisely because she would have to pay for them with long days and nights of worry — worry that she might suddenly lose that which she had ventured so much to gain, worry that it all might one day suddenly be over and the gold of happiness nothing but withered leaves and she herself lonelier and poorer than ever before. This worry never left her, he knew that. Once — it was not that long ago — they'd arranged to meet at his flat. The hour approached and he was waiting for her; then the doorbell rang and he hurried to answer: but it wasn't her, it was one of his friends who'd dropped by for a chat. He could hardly have replied that he was busy, or that he was expecting a visitor, because his friend would have run into her on the way downstairs and the game would have been up; instead he said that he was just on the way out to deal with some urgent business, threw on a coat and hat and they went out together. Not long out of the front door he saw her coming down the street; she fixed him with an uncertain and frightened look and he greeted her in passing, politely and somewhat distancingly, as he had to so as not to betray her. He turned into a side street to be rid of the friend, and after a few minutes' detour arrived back at his front door. She was walking round outside, in the rain and the dirt. He softly pressed her hand and they went up to his flat together; but when they got inside he saw she was shaking with tears.

No explanations were necessary — she'd already worked out what was going on — but his curt, cool passing greeting, as he chatted with some unknown gentleman, was enough to drive all these secret fears coursing through her veins, and she had to have air, she had to cry, and she cried long and silently in his arms.

Much, indeed, had it given them, this meagre happiness of theirs, but the cold clear light of language it could not bear, it did not fare well being spoken of. The whole of his tenderness could not present her with the ease that comes from a life that can be lived in front of the crowds and approved by them, nor could it prevent her, sometimes when alone, from feeling shame and pangs of conscience. For, since life had shown her two faces, which she could not reconcile, she had not one conscience but two. One told her that she had acted rightly and that there would come a time when nobody would understand how it could once have been that love between a man and a woman might be enveloped in dirt and shame and called a sin. But the other said nothing about the future: it rose up from the depths of the past, speaking with the voice of her dead mother and with voices from her home in the woods and from her childhood when she knew nothing about the world or about herself, when everything was simple and you needed only be nice and all was well. And in the evenings when he'd just left her and she was sitting alone in her rented flat surrounded by somebody else's tasteless furniture — the dresser with its Empire mirror and green marble top was the only thing of hers and the only thing to remind her of her childhood home — this old conscience rose up and whispered many nasty things in her ears. It whispered that those women who marry loathsome men so they can be provided for, and those wretched girls who sell their bodies because they have to, are both better than she: for at least they had a reason and she had none. And it did not help to think of her great love, and defend herself with it: the old conscience knew that trick well enough and it whispered back that it wasn't he who'd lit the fire in her blood, it was her own desire that stoked it, and that the evil was within her, and she was a wanton creature who ought to be whipped at the stake with birch rods as they used to do with loose women in days gone by. And her conscience found even worse things to whisper in her ear: it whispered that the man she loved would soon tire of her, indeed, that he had already tired of her, and that in his heart he despised her because she was always so ready to sin and had never denied him anything.

He knew all this, for she always shared her worries with him. And always this way of thinking left him bewildered and confused: that the same desire, which in a man is so natural and simple and as easy to admit to as thirst or hunger, is in a woman a burning shame that must be stifled or concealed. It was a notion he had never been able to fathom emotionally, though intellectually he might be able to trace it back to its origins far off in the mists of the most ancient times, when a woman was still a man's property and when her sensuality was admissible and indeed laudable insofar as it gave expression to her subordination to her master's will, but shameful and criminal when it arose from her own. And so deeply rooted is this notion in the hearts of men that in books as in life one can but rarely hear a man speak of a woman's tender desire other than with derision and ridicule — at least so far as it does not pertain to him himself and his own desires, and often not even then. And so deeply does it still attach to women's minds that modest women not uncommonly feel a secret shame that they love their husbands and long for their embrace. Indeed, Martin recalled how he'd once even heard a common street girl dividing her kind into the decent and the sluttish: and by the decent she meant those who only thought of the money. And in fact this division was truer and deeper than even she realised; it had its origin in an economics of womanhood passed on from one generation to the next over millennia; necessity had dictated it from the beginning, the necessity of preventing generosity and profligacy from undercutting the price of that good which was the only asset of the weaker and the one thing that could save her from utter subordination to the stronger. And if that poor street girl had been a little better up in the Bible she could have invoked the prophet Ezekiel in support of her distinction, with his frenzied denunciation of the wanton Oholah, who was not like other whores, 'whom one has to buy with money'.

He understood all this perfectly well; life was too parsimonious to allow women to go for free, and he didn't condemn any of them, not even the respectable ones. But he was fond of his bounteous girlfriend and comforted her as best he could on those days when the conflicting voices within her had frightened her and filled her with anxiety: which was easy for him, because when he was with her she felt no fear. But he knew too that there were days, indeed weeks, in which she went in an all-consuming fear lest she have conceived a child, despite everything. And he did not conceal from himself that this was the tainted part of all secret love. He saw plainly how loaded the dice always were in everything hereabouts, how all the danger and the risk fell on the woman, and once more he felt a secret shame that it was beyond his power to share what was bitter with her, as he shared the sweet. The risk of conceiving a child was first and foremost hers, and if that peril were successfully avoided then the absence and the emptiness of being unable to allow herself the joys of motherhood was hers too; and his heart cut when once in the street at twilight he saw her take a stranger's child in her arms and kiss her. But with the world as it was motherhood would have entailed a terrible misery for her.

But neither of them had been spoiled by life. They both had learned not to long for an immaculate happiness, and their love had helped them take all this as it must and should be taken.

She was ready now. She extinguished the candles in front of the mirror and waited in the dark for a few minutes while he went down to the street before her, so that no one should encounter them together on the staircase. Outside, on the street, they dared to walk together once it was dark, especially if the air were misty, or in rain or snow. And on this evening the snow fell so thick and white that no one would have been able to recognise them. Like shadows, anonymous and without distinction, people glided past them in the white night; and anonymous themselves, huddled tight together, vaguely resembling the yoked couples that children cut out of folded paper, they made their way on through the snow. She held his arm pressed against her breast, and they both were silent.

5

It was dark in the auditorium, and Martin had opened the shutters in the trelliswork. Nobody could see them, nor, from where he was sitting in his corner, could he see anything of what happened onstage; he just heard verses and lines of dialogue emanating into the darkness and observed, or fancied he observed, their effect on the pale masks of human faces along the arced rows of the stalls — a sloping flower bed full of large, strange blooms, etiolated as plants become when they live without the sun, and not precisely beautiful as they slowly shifted as under a silent wind or suddenly nodded now and then on their stems.

He seemed to recognise them all, either because by now he really had run into them so often, on the great stages of the city streets and the restaurants and cafés, where he, like them, was another extra, that their faces had persisted in his memory without his knowing it; or because people's faces tended to belong to one of a small number of different types, so that one rarely feels one has encountered a truly new face.

And moreover, he seemed to know some of these faces very well. Over there was Henrik Rissler, friend from his earliest youth. They rarely met nowadays, which was a pity, because there was no one Martin knew who better appreciated friendship, thought and cigars than he. But he was married now, had been for several years, and was forever on the move. He'd not yet reached the end of the young couple's eternal odyssey from one mouldy flat to another, always in the suburbs, from Vasastaden to Söder, from Söder to Kungsholmen. But Martin had a feeling that life would bring them together once again, if only each could find a little more peace.

And there, a little way further down, that little furrowed face, a bit like a child's and a bit like an old man's too, wasn't that another old schoolmate, wasn't that Josef Marin? He never did become a priest, as he'd meant to to oblige his stubborn old mother. He was never secure in his faith. Now, it's probably often true that faith is like appetite, which can come in the course of a meal; but he'd never reached the point where the eating actually begins; moreover, at heart he'd perhaps a thirst for honesty that would make such a path a bit too troublesome. Now he wrote entertainment reviews and obituaries for an important newspaper. He pulled no punches expressing his opinions, and he took pains to have the same opinions he thought his editor had; and his editor, a veritable firebrand of a freethinker, always strove to have the thoughts he imagined wealthy and educated people in general had. And because these principles had always been the ruling ones at the newspaper, it's become much loved and respected and highly venerable and has acquired a solid reputation for impeccable propriety and impartial truth seeking.

"Actually, I could just as well have become a priest," he'd

said to Martin one day, a little wistfully, as they exchanged a few words on a street corner.

. . . And there, high up at the back, that slender fair-skinned woman, wasn't that the woman he'd longed for on those spring nights many years ago, Harriet Skotte? He'd written a letter to her that he'd never sent, hadn't he? Oh yes, those days . . . It seemed things had gone a little awry for her since then: she did not look happy. She was married now, and her husband was sitting by her side. He was rather stout and very expensively dressed and looked as if he'd been varnished. Poor dear girl, she isn't thriving with that estimable gentleman, it's plain from the look of him . . .

And he saw other faces, women whom he knew a little, though they didn't know him, young women he'd fond memories of because one time or other, without knowing it, they'd made him a little richer and happier by sailing past him on the street like sunlit clouds . . . Down there was one he recognised very well, because she'd once noticed his admiring gaze, wrapped her skirts tight round her and given him a look as if he were Jack the Ripper. Poor lady, time passes, she's no longer young — even then she was past the peak of ripeness, and she probably doesn't get eyed when she walks down Sturegatan any more . . .

Martin had grown tired of listening to one thing and looking at another; the strange, profound old words sounding out from the stage meant nothing to him at this moment; and it seemed to him, reading the masks down there in the stalls, that the words were bouncing back unheard from them too, and that they scarcely grasped anything of what was happening onstage beyond the pure theatrics.

They were in the fifth act already, and Martin leaned back in his corner and let the two gravediggers trade skulls and witticisms as pleased them best, and sought his girlfriend's eyes in the darkness. But he couldn't meet them, for she could see everything from where she sat and didn't take her eyes off the stage. And once more the words came vividly to life in his ears, seeing the excitement in her face; and the entire grave-yard scene, which he knew so well but couldn't see, he fancied he saw mirrored in her eyes. He saw Hamlet standing there in his cloak of night and riddles, and with Yorick's skull in his hand; he saw the funeral procession, the coffin being lowered, and the Queen strewing flowers in the grave: 'Sweets to the sweet!' He saw the strange goings on in the grave, the two men fighting down there, and he heard Hamlet's voice: 'I loved Ophelia!'

What does he want? Does he want to snatch her up out of the grave? Suppose she weren't dead, suppose she rose now out of the coffin, awake and rosy-cheeked after a peaceful sleep — would he take her in his arms and carry her off and love her till the end of days? No: that's not what he means. When she was still alive he told her: 'I did love you once.' Now certainly he was no regular Don Juan, he'd not forgotten her for another lady-in-waiting with a narrower waistline and bigger breasts, yet still he could tell her: 'I did love you once.' He could per-haps say that about a lot of things. He'd also loved the sun and the flowers and the trees. The blue sky too he'd loved, and fire and water and the good earth. He'd loved all these things; to all four elements and to life itself he might have said: 'I did love you once.' But since then something changed, something crept in between him and all these things, something that took him in its power without asking permission and drove all the other things away, the sun and the flowers and women and that woman, far, far away so that he scarcely saw them any more, except as through a fog . . . And now, seeing the funeral pro-cession coming and hearing that she, the one whom he'd loved, was being buried, he suddenly recalled what once he had had, and lost; but he knew too that he'd lost her and everything else long before she was dead, and the loss itself appeared real to him only in that first moment, in the next it too he perceived from far away, as if through a fog . . .

Martin had closed his eyes, and when he opened them again he himself saw everything as if through a fog: the stalls and the white masks down there, and she, whom he loved. And she took his hand and caressed it gently between her two warm hands and whispered to him, "What were you thinking about?"

# 6

The winter night was sleeping all around them. It was no longer snowing; they walked home through the drifts in a white moonlit mist, went in through the street door and up the stairway towards her flat. The higher they rose, the brighter it grew. They stopped by a window, bathed in a flood of moonlight, and looked out. The mist lay mostly beneath them now, swept out over courtyards and gardens, but higher up the air was almost clear, bluish and bright like an August night. A broad bright ring circled the moon, and in the pale light the world lay frozen, petrified, and out of the sea of fog below rose a solitary windowless gable end, sucking in the moon's cold gaze and staring back, blind and empty. A shiver ran through them both, and with closed eyes they pressed together tight, and all was lost to them in a kiss. It was a long, wondrous kiss. He felt the whole of his being dissolve, and in his ears he heard a ringing of bells, remotely, as from a little village church far away, among meadows and cornfields. It was like a Sunday morning, and he saw a sandy square neatly raked, peonies shone red from gardens, white and yellow butterflies fluttered among the bushes and grasses, and he heard the whispering of great trees. He was walking with her among them, but through the canopies' whispering there blew a gust of autumn, and the yellow butterflies were yellow leaves, and already some were blackened by frosts. The wind brought with it fragments of melody and words, like the mundane words of everyday speech but no less like stolen whispers of a secret that must be kept, and it mingled with them like an echo of the strange intonation in the actor's voice when he said, 'I loved Ophelia!' But he didn't leave off kissing her, and they sank ever deeper into one another, and he seemed to be journeying through space, and in the moon-white mist a red star shone, at first dim and fading, then brighter and ever closer, growing, broadening to a blazing fount of flame, and with his lips he clung fast to it. And he felt himself burning without pain, the flames slaked his tongue like a tart wine; and everything, satiety and hunger, thirst and slaking, the vigour of the sun and the anguish of darkness, the cool thoughts of the day and the moon-haunted brooding of night, all the world's joy and all its misery he seemed to drink from this fount.

Also by Hjalmar Söderberg, translated by David Barrett:

*Doctor Glas*

*Diversions*

Printed in Great Britain
by Amazon